THE LEFT HANDED GUN

TONY MONTE

iUniverse, Inc.
Bloomington

The Left-Handed Gun

This is a work of fiction. All of the characters, names, incidents, organizations, and dialogue in this novel are either the products of the author's imagination or are used fictitiously.

iUniverse books may be ordered through booksellers or by contacting:

iUniverse
1663 Liberty Drive
Bloomington, IN 47403
www.iuniverse.com
1-800-Authors (1-800-288-4677)

ISBN: 978-1-4502-8847-7 (sc)
ISBN: 978-1-4502-8849-1 (dj)
ISBN: 978-1-4502-8848-4 (ebook)

Printed in the United States of America

iUniverse rev. date: 01/13/2011

CHAPTER 1

JOHN HEADS WEST

Young John Cole rode into the town of Abilene, in Kansas. The day was hot, very hot. The year was 1879. His bay mare was as tired and worn as he was. He spoke softly to his horse, "It will not be long now Amber, and you can rest and get some oats". To his right were the stockyards, a sign read Joseph G. McCoy Proprietor. There were a number of water troughs along the fence. John dismounted next to one and let Amber have a drink, while he splashed water over his hot and dusty face. A young boy was playing in the road with a stick and his dog. "Boy where is the stable?" The boy looked up, "Crenshaw's, down at the very end of the street and to the left" he said. John mounted and gave a slight jab with his spurs. His horse plodded forward, the horse must have smelled the stable, for it picked up the pace on its own. John looked around at the buildings, a hotel and a bank that looked as if you could break into it with a crowbar. John turned left down the first rutted dusty street; He saw the stable on the left and the saloon across on the right. He stopped in front of the open door of the stable and dismounted, He looked at the dirty old man sitting in a chair. "Are you the stableman?"

"That be me sonny, Crenshaw's the name."

John asked "How much to board my horse Crenshaw?"

"Two bits a day" grunted Crenshaw. John flipped him a quarter, "Grain, and rub him down."

"You are somewhat young to be barking orders," Crenshaw said. Cole gave him a hard stare. The old man looked at the tied down gun, "Ok I will take good care of him." Cole looked around, saw the Buffalo saloon, and walked across the rutted street, stepped up onto the porch and pushed open the batwing doors. Cole waited for his eyes to adjust to the dark room; he walked over to the bar and laid a nickel on polished wood, "Beer." There were two men on his left at the bar and an old man to his right. Behind the bar there was a mirror on the wall and a shelf with whiskey bottles. Looking in the mirror, John saw some men sitting at tables staring at him. Turning his head around, John said, "A man does not like to be stared at when he is drinking." John noticed they looked at his tied down gun, and then looked the other way.

The man at the end of the bar said, "You don't look old enough to drink." Cole picked up the glass with his right hand, took a sip of the warm beer, stared at the man, and then said. "And you might get older if you mind your own business." "Just making talk young man, did not mean to rile you." Cole finished up his beer. He turned back to the bar. "Where can I get a bed?" Cole asked the bartender."

"Go left out the door, across the street and four doors down. Gus said; "The Abilene Hotel."

Cole picked up his saddlebags, and tossed them over his right shoulder, then picked up his dads' old rifle, and left the bar. He then walked to the hotel, looking over the town as he went, entering the dimly lit hotel; he again waited for his eyes to adjust. Cole walked over to the desk clerk. "I want a room facing the street."

"That will be two bits a day. Room two, on the right." Cole gave him two bits, signed the register, picked up the key and turned towards the stairs. Cole walked up the stairs, and walked over to the room marked 2, he tried the door, it was unlocked, with his is left hand on his gun, He pushed the door open with his right hand, looking around to make sure no one was in the room. He entered the small shabby room, locked the door, and looked around. It was a typical hotel room. It had a bed, small washbasin, kerosene lamp, old curtains hanging limply on the one dusty window and a pitcher of water on the worn old table. He dropped his saddlebags on the floor and rested his rifle against the old dresser; He took off his gun, laid it on the bed, and then lay down close to it. He closed his tired eyes, and thought back of his family. He thought of his Mother and Father, and his older brother Bill. Who already had a reputation as the fastest gun alive, But John knew there was one faster..

CHAPTER 2
WAGON'S WEST

John thought back to the small farm they had in Ohio, He had sold the few cattle, about ten head, it was a farm and ranch combined, about a hundred and sixty acres. Though he was only fifteen, he had to do a man's work, for his father and mother; both in their seventies were sick and not long for this world. John thought back to his Father telling how they came to Ohio.

William Cole was born in 1808 along the Hudson River, In the Eastern Kaatskil Mountains. At the age of eighteen, he married his lifelong girlfriend, Mira O'Leary. Not being able to make a decent living, William took his new bride and headed west with all his possessions. Two horses and a pack mule, loaded with all the food they could carry and his old Flintlock rifle and pistol. Not being a talkative man, William did not tell his sons much about the trip to Ohio. When Bill was 13 and John 10, they were sitting in the cabin at the dinner table. The cabin had two rooms with a loft, where the boys slept. John asked; "Pa on your way here from New York, did you have to kill any injuns?" Even now he could hear his father talking to him.

"John, killing another human being is not a good thing, but sometimes a man has to do things, he does not like. It is not the way of the Lord, to kill. I will tell you of one instance. After making camp one night, we ate our meager dinner of bread and beans, and then we turned in for the night.

Sometime close to morning, I was woken, by the braying of the mule. I pulled off my blankets and grabbed my rifle." Young John with both arms on the table, mouth open, listened intently.

"I saw someone leading the mule away; we could not afford to lose the mule. I had no choice! I brought the rifle to my shoulder and shot the man. I took my powder horn, and shot pouch and reloaded my rifle. I did not know how many were around. Lucky for us it was one, lone Indian. I wondered why he was trying to take the mule, and not the horses. Later I found out they like mule meat. There were a few more problems along the way. About a week later, I saw smoke off in the distance, fearing it might be Indians, I told your mother we would make camp and lay low for the rest of the day. The next morning we had a cold breakfast, I was afraid to attract attention to ourselves. As your mother packed the mule, I saddled the two horses and we headed where we saw the smoke. After climbing a rise we saw a burnt out wagon, near the wagon we saw three forms, I knew right away what they were. "When we got close enough where I could still keep an eye on your mother, I told her to stay back with the mule. I could smell the stench of death and so could my horse, as he became hard to control. I dismounted and ground hitched him, taking my rifle with me I approached the bodies. There was a man, woman and a young girl, all were dead, and had been mutilated. It was all I could do not to lose my cold breakfast. There was not much of anything left. The Indians took almost everything. I saw a Bible lying next to the woman, it was in bad shape, but I could make out the family's names. Cian Moore, Shannon and Erin Moore and their birth dates, I can't remember the dates, but the young girl was only ten that I will always remember. There were still some scraps of clothing thrown around, so I gathered what I could and wrapped the bodies in them the best I could, as I did this I realized how foolish I was to try and make this trip alone. But it was too late to turn back now, I did not fear for myself, but I feared for your mom."

"After I had the bodies covered, I waved for your mom to come to me. I found a piece of board that I could dig with and started digging, your mom rode up and dismounted and helped me the best she could, we had to bury them all together, we did the best we could. Your mom prayed the "23rd Psalm, "Yea though I walk through the valley of death I fear no evil, for thou art with me." We then walked the horses all over the grave;

packing the earth so no animals could find it and dig it up. As we were doing that I thought, "I hope no one will be praying over us." "Then I heard riders coming, fearing they were Indian, I hid your mom under the burnt out wagon covering her with anything I could find. I then waited behind my horse with my rifle over the saddle, four men came over the knoll, I thanked the Lord they were white men. I lowered my rifle and they rode up and dismounted. They said they were from a wagon train about two miles away, seeing the smoke they came to see what it was. I believed they were friendly, so I went and got your mom. They told me I was crazy to try and reach Ohio alone and said we could join the wagon train. That we did, I wished the Moore's could have been as lucky as we were. I helped your mom on her horse, mounted mine and with the mule behind me on a lead rope we followed the men to the wagon train. Upon reaching the wagon train, one of the men introduced us to the wagon master.

"Mr. Murphy this is the Cole family, heading for Ohio, I told them they should join us."

"Howdy folks, Craig Murphy is the name, where is your wagon". "Pleased to meet you Mr. Murphy, we have no wagon."

"Mrs. Clemons lost her husband a ways back, I'm sure she would welcome your help driving her wagon". We followed Mr. Murphy to the wagon train, where he introduced us to Mrs. Clemons, She was a pretty lady but she seemed kind of frail to me. It made me wonder why a man would take a woman like her west. As I later learned, Mr. Clemons should have stayed in the east also; his death was an accident, but a very stupid one. After making camp one night, he decided to practice with his new rifle, it appears he put the cap on the rifle first, and then cocked the hammer, and with the butt of the rifle on the ground, he poured the powder down the barrel and tamped the ball home. Well the hammer let loose and the ball took Mr. Clemons in the head. Some people have no common sense and should never touch a gun. Sad to say Mr. Clemons was one of them. I looked her wagon and mules over; everything looked in good shape, but having one more would not hurt. You're Mom and Mrs. Clemons got along very good. This made the trip much easier for your mom and me. "Well boys that is enough, the rest of the trip was not that exciting, just a lot of hard work and that's what is planned for us today, a lot of hard work.

CHAPTER 3

BOYHOOD DREAMS

The next morning William looked at John. "I have taught Bill how to shoot. I think John; it is time for you to learn, the west is a very dangerous place. You can trust no one you don't know." "Tomorrow, after your chores, we will do some shooting; it is about time you learn." John was so excited he could hardly sleep. He was up before the dawn. Grabbing his clothes and boots, being as quiet as he could John climbed down the ladder and got dressed. He walked to the door and went out. He looked towards the east; the sun was just starting to rise. He went over to the corral, pitched hay to the horses and the mule, grabbed the bucket, ran to the pump and filled the bucket with water. John then brought the bucket to the door of the house, he ran to the barn opened the big door, grabbed a bucket and a stool, sat down and milked the cow. Hurrying to the house John carefully put the milk near the door. All that was left of the morning chores was to chop wood. John grabbed the ax and started splitting wood. His father walked out the door. "John," his father said; "How many times do we have to tell you to use your right hand?" Without saying a word, John switched the ax to his right hand, Left, right, either hand made no difference to him.

Bill walked out the door. "Well Bill" his father said; "looks like you got lucky this morning, young John did all the chores. Go get the rifle, pistol and shot pouch." Bill had shot the guns and hunted with them so

7

many times that he was in no hurry. After a few minutes, that seemed like an hour to John. Bill came out of the house with the pistol in his belt and shot pouch hanging over his shoulder and the rifle in his hand. John was walking in the lead. Father and sons walked to the back of the barn. There was a big rock, about fifty feet away. Cans were lying all around the rock, where Bill had done his shooting. "Bill" his father said; "put up some cans." He then handed John the pistol. Bill hollered; "Wait till I get out of here."

John raised the pistol with his left hand. His Father said; "How many times do I have to tell you to use your right hand" John started to switch hands, His father said; "Forget it shoot with the hand that is more comfortable for you." "Shooting is a serious thing, if you can shoot better with your left, then its better you use it."

It took John five shots before he could hit the can. John reloaded the pistol. Bill took the pistol from John, whipped around brought the gun up, cocked it, fired and hit the can. "Ok let John try the rifle" his father said. "The rifle is loaded; always remember to reload after you shoot." John raised the heavy flintlock to his shoulder, pulled back the hammer, took aim at the can and squeezed the trigger. Wham, it kicked back against his shoulder. The next thing John knew, he was sitting on his ass. At ten John was a small boy. His father and Bill were trying not to laugh. "Well boys, I think mom has breakfast ready." John used his right hand to eat breakfast, without being told to, for his left shoulder hurt like hell.

That night while in bed, Bill and John talked about how exciting it would be to go farther west. Bill told John: "I am saving every penny I can get my hands on, to buy a pistol and holster, I carved a gun out of wood, and I practice every chance I get. Someday I am going to be the fastest gun alive."

"I would not let dad hear you say that."

"I won't, and don't you say anything. I plan on heading west in a few more years." "Can I go with you?" John asked

"No you will be too young, and Mom and Dad will need you here." John gritted his teeth and said, "I'm not going to be a farmer all my life either." Bill told him, "When the time is right you can join me, we will be the feared, Cole brothers." They both fell asleep dreaming of the west and of being gunfighters.

~ CHAPTER 4 ~
BILL HEADS WEST

Bill Cole said goodbye to his mom, dad and brother John; He had just turned eighteen, he was already a year behind his boyhood dream to head west and become a famous gunfighter.

Being true to what he told his brother John; he had saved every penny he could get his hands on. It was time to buy a gun and a horse. Keith Morgan was the closest rancher and always had horses for sale; it was a five-mile walk.

Upon reaching the Morgan Ranch, he could not help being envious of the spread, and all the horses in the coral, he looked them over as he headed for the sprawling ranch house, then he started worrying he would not have enough money for a horse and a pistol.

As Bill was stepping on the porch, Mr. Morgan came out the door, "Hello Bill Cole, what brings you here?"

"Hello Mr. Morgan, I would like to buy a horse, if I can afford one."

"Well Bill I have three that are getting on in years, still good horses, You can take your pick for thirty dollars and I will throw in a bridle."

"I would like that Dapple Gray."

"Well he's yours then."

Bill reached in his pocket and took out thirty dollars and handed it to Morgan, "Thanks Mr. Morgan."

"Can I ask where you are heading Bill?"

"I have wanted to see some of the west for a long time now, Mr. Morgan; I have been saving every penny I could get my hands on."

"You don't seem to be too well outfitted, Bill You don't even have a gun, and there is a lot of danger out there."

"I know, I am going to buy a gun and supplies in town, my dad did teach me how to shoot, but he only has the one pistol."

"Well I have an old cap and ball pistol, and holster for it, I could let you have it for, say five dollars."

"If you have some powder, shot and caps for it, I will buy it.

"Sit tight I will get it for you."

A few minutes later Morgan came out with the gun. "Here you go Bill, it is still in good shape and shoots true, just be careful with it." Bill thanked him and counted out the five dollars.

Bill mounted the gray and headed for town, A few miles from the Morgan ranch, he stopped, dismounted and tried out his new gun. As Mr. Morgan said, the gun shot true.

He practiced drawing the gun; he was smooth and fairly fast with it. Feeling pleased with himself he headed for town.

After buying what he needed he headed west, he wanted to get as far as Texas. The day was more than half gone, so he decided to make camp for the night at a small creek he knew of. Upon reaching the creek, he saw two men setting up camp.

He hollered "Hello." and rode into the camp. Two dirty and scraggily dressed men looked at him, one said; "Well did you ever see such a seed head in your life, har, har."

Bill could see trouble coming, "Sorry to bother you men, I will be on my way."

One of the men grabbed the bridle on his horse "Not so fast boy, what ya got in them bags."

"Mr. Let go of my horse."

"And what if I don't boy?"

With a fast and smooth draw, his gun was out, cocked and pointed at the man's chest. The man let go in a hurry, Bill kept his gun on the man, as he reined his horse around, "Don't cause me anymore trouble or I will kill you." Then he rode off to make camp further down the creek.

About a mile down the creek he made his camp, knowing he had not seen the last of them, Bill cooked some food, then after eating he fixed his bed for the night, when the fire was down to just coals, he went and hid behind a large pine tree, waiting for the two brothers.

About midnight, they approached his camp, without a word they both shot into his bedroll. Bill did not say anything either, he took careful aim like his dad taught him and shot the first man in the middle of the chest, then did the same to the other.

He then walked over and checked to see if both men were dead, they both had robbed their last man.

The one that had done all the talking had a nice Colt 44, so Bill took the pistol, holster and all the ammo they had. Then looked for their horses, they were about a hundred feet away, tied to some scrub trees, Bill decided to take the best saddle for himself . After he unsaddled the one he did not want, he turned the horse loose, and led the other to his camp, "No sense carrying this saddle when I got you." When he reached his camp, he unsaddled the horse and let it go also. Talking out loud, "Dead men don't need guns or saddles."

And so began Bill Cole's journey west to a new life as a Gunfighter and Lawman.

— CHAPTER 5 —

BILL COMES HOME

John had sent letters to Buffalo Gap, the county seat and as far as Nacogdoches trying to find his brother to tell him their parents had died. Bill was well known and feared as a gunfighter and the last John had heard he was a Sheriff somewhere in Texas.

John walked behind the old mule and plow he wanted to get the field ready to plant corn. A movement across the plains caught his eye; he looked and saw a lone man riding toward him. John kept plowing, keeping a watch on the stranger as the rider got closer he realized it was his brother Bill. John unhitched the mule, and rode out to meet his brother.

As they came closer, "I see you finally read my letters, you're a year late." John said:

Bill had a sad look on his face. "I came as soon as I got word."

John said, "Well you must be tired and hungry, let's get some food." When they got to the house, Bill asked; "Where are they buried?" John pointed to the old big oak tree. Bill dismounted and walked slowly up the hill to the old tree. John took the horse to the barn; he unsaddled, grained and watered the horse, then went into the house and started supper. A while later Bill came into the house, sat at the table, and started eating the food his brother put before him. Bill asked, "Are you going to stay and work the place?"

John shook his head "No, I was planning to get a crop in, and then sell everything. I want to get away from here and see some of the country." Bill said, "It is a hard and dangerous country out there. "Do you have a gun?"

"I have the old Winchester that was Pa's."

Bill said; "I have a spare colt 44; tomorrow I will teach you how to use it." The sun was down and the brothers were tired, they turned in for the night.

CHAPTER 6

THE FIRST LESSON

At dawn, they had their breakfast of coffee, bread and ham. Bill asked; "Are you ready for your first lesson"? John nodded. They went out behind the barn, where their dad had taught them how to shoot the old rifle and pistol. Bill handed John his spare colt. "This is not like the old cap and ball that dad had us shoot. It holds six shots and uses center fire cartridges." Bill showed him how to load and shoot the colt. John was a natural with a gun; in no time at all he could shoot as good as Bill.

Bill said, "I forgot that you are left handed. We will have to fix that holster for you." John said nothing to Bill, but thought how his mother and father always scolded him for using his left hand. He smiled as he thought back. John eat with your right hand, hammer with your right hand. People will think you are odd if you are left-handed. John was just as comfortable with either hand, but preferred his left hand. The days passed quickly, plowing and practicing with the gun. John was amazed at how fast Bill could draw and hit the target. But by the end of summer, John was as fast, if not faster than Bill.

Bill took two old bean cans gave one to John. "Put one on the fence post and move a few feet away from it"

Bill walked about twenty feet away, and put the empty can on the fence post next to him.

"There is one thing I cannot teach you, either you have it or you don't."
John asked "What is that?"

"Very few men can tell when a man is about to go for his gun, if you
can tell this, it will give you a big edge. As for myself I do not have it, I
have to watch the hand. Let's see if you have it, but remember to shoot
the dam can and not me." John laughed and said he would try. They stood
watching each other, Bill watching John's hand, John watching Bills eyes.
John knew when Bill decided it was time to draw, a split second before he
went for his gun, John drew and shot the can, Bills gun was barely out of
his holster. John could tell that Bill was shaken, for no one had ever beaten
him before, his being alive proved that. Bill shook his head, "looks like you
got it, if you were not my brother I would be dead now, I taught you all I
can, all you can do now is practice. The more you practice the better you
will get. The only other advice I can give you, is don't look for trouble, it
will find you easy enough. One thing more, if you have to draw on a man,
shoot to kill, don't even think about it. Always aim for the biggest target,
the chest."

The next morning, Bill said he had to get back to his job, as sheriff.
"Here is where you can reach me," and handed him the slip of paper, with
the address. Bill mounted his red roan said goodbye to his brother and
rode away.

Yawning, John settled down to sleep, He had not heard from his
brother since he left. That was two years ago.

CHAPTER 7

SHORTY'S CHALLENGE

The sun was just rising when John woke up, the first thing he did every morning was strap on his gun, then washed his face, and then went down stairs. At the desk he asked where a good place to eat was. "Mary's place, three doors down on the left" was the clerk's reply. He thanked him and stepped out the door, almost colliding with the sheriff. John nodded and went to step around the big man, but the sheriff stopped in front of him blocking the exit.

"Is there a problem, Sheriff?"

"No problem, I just like to see what brings strangers to my town."

"Well not to worry sheriff, I will only be staying a few days."

"That is good to hear, but when a man wears a gun like you do, and his name is Cole. There are always problems."

John looked him in the eyes, "I do not look for trouble sheriff, but I do not run either."

"That is good to hear, but."

"You have a lot of buts' Sheriff."

"Well Cole we have some young men here that figure they are good with a gun, and I do not want any gunfights."

"Well go tell them that. Now if you do not mind I would like to have some breakfast." he stepped around the sheriff, and walked down the dusty street to Mary's Place. The restaurant was empty. There were several tables covered white cloths. John walked over to one and sat down. A young and very pretty girl walked over to take his order. Cole looked up into the bluest eyes he had ever seen. "Are you Mary he asked?"

"No Mary is my mother. My name is Jenny."

"Well Jenny, if I may call you that, I would like coffee, ham, and eggs."

She smiled and said. "Coming right up", and walked back to the kitchen. John could not take his eyes off her. Even though she was gone for only a short time, to John it seemed like hours, for he wanted to see her again. She smiled at him and placed his food on the table. Looking at Jenny, he thought, I might stay longer than a few days. He ate his breakfast very slow hoping to see her again. He put two bits on the table, got up, and walked towards the door.

Jenny called after him "I hope you enjoyed your breakfast, Mr.?"

John turned; "John Cole, but call me John, Jenny."

She smiled; "Dinners served at six John."

"I will see you then Jenny." John felt there was something familiar about her, but could not put his finger on it. Jenny watched John leave then walked into the kitchen. Her mom said; "You seem to be taken by that young man."

"Mom I think that is John Cole from Ohio," She paused, "No, I am sure of it, you remember the Cole's, Bill and John; they used to call me pigtail"

Mary stopped drying the dishes; "I do remember the Cole's, William and Mira. But I did not get a good look at the young man." As Jenny washed the dishes, she thought back to when she was a young girl. Always following Bill and John around, she remembered that she had a crush on John. She would go fishing, and roughhouse with them. They never called her Jenny; they always called her pigtail. She wondered if they ever even knew her real name. She smiled; well John is looking at me a little different now. Will he be surprised, if I ever tell him?

Cole walked over to the telegraph office. He told the clerk, "I want to send a telegraph, to Bill Cole the Sheriff of Adobe Walls." The clerk handed him a pencil and paper and told him to write it down, "A penny a letter he told him." Cole wrote the message down handed it to the clerk.

WILL COME IF NEED ME - STOP - JOHN.

The clerk read the telegram." That will be twenty-four-cents." Cole counted out the coins, "I will be back later to check for a return message." Cole walked down the dusty street that had not seen rain for over a month, taking in the sights of the town as he went. It was a typical town, stores, saddle shops, saloons and eating places. John had a real thirst so he headed for the first saloon he saw; the sign said Gus's Place. John pushed the double bat winged doors open, and then stepped inside, waiting for his eyes to adjust to the dark room. He walked over to the bar and laid a nickel on the polished wood, "Cold beer."

Cole picked the beer up with his right hand took a sip and looked around the room. Two young men, not as young as himself, maybe a few years older, were looking at him. The short one said; "You do not look old enough to be a famous gunfighter to me." Not wanting trouble, Cole said; "That's because I'm not."

"You wear that gun like you are."

"I wear mine the same as you. Are you a famous gunfighter?"

"Not yet but I plan to be."

"Good luck" and He sipped his warm beer. Shorty hitched up his gun belt, "Are you trying to say I will not be?"

John was getting a little pissed off, "All I am trying to do is drink a beer, so why don't you just leave me be."

"Is Bill Cole your brother?"

Cole set his beer down on the bar, turned and faced Shorty "Who I am has nothing to do with you. Now mind your own business and let me alone."

Smirking Shorty said, "What if I don't want to leave you alone?" Cole turned and faced the big mouth. "Ok, Bill Cole is my brother;

He taught me all he could. Now let it go."

CHAPTER 8

JOHN'S FIRST GUNFIGHT

"I think you are just a scared kid that is full of cow shit."

Cole looked at Shorty "I don't want to kill you, but if it's a fight you want, pull your gun!"

Cole looked into Shorty's eyes and knew he was going to draw. Shorty just got his hand on his gun, when Cole shot him in the middle of his chest. Shorty dropped his gun, putting both hands over his chest, then fell over backwards and knew no more.

John heard a man at the bar say, If I didn't see it with my own eyes, I would not believe it, the gun just seemed to appear in his hand, it was almost too fast to see. Cole looked at Shorty's friend. Shorty's friend shook his head, "Not me mister."

John ejected the spent .44 and replaced it with a new one. He picked up his beer, and tried to keep his hands from shaking, as he took a big swallow. John knew the town sheriff would be there soon. He was right, within a minute the sheriff came in, looked at the dead man and then at Cole. "I just knew it would be you."

Gus the bartender said. "Shorty started it and drew first Pete, He pointed to Cole, this gentleman tried to avoid it. Shorty gave him no choice."

The marshal looked at Cole. "Just the same, I want you out of town."

Cole was angry, "You heard the bartender, I have the right to defend myself. I will leave when I am ready." The sheriff lowered his hand towards his holster; Cole looked the sheriff in the eyes. "Don't do it sheriff, I just killed one man. And I did not like it." The sheriff moved his hand away from his gun. "I will make it easy for you sheriff, I am waiting for a telegraph message, when it arrives, I will be gone."

The sheriff nodded, turned to Shorty's friend, "He was your friend, get him over to the undertaker, then turned and left." Cole was shaken by the gunfight, but finished his beer.

Gus looked at Cole, "I killed a man once, it bothered me for a long time, but you had no choice. He would have killed you." Gus gave Cole another beer, "This one is on the house."

Cole thanked him and said; "Why do they all want to be the fastest?"

Gus asked, "Why you want to be the fastest?"

"I don't, but with a name like Cole, I have to be."

Cole did not know why, but for some reason he wanted to see Jenny. He walked to the door, looked out and waited for his eyes to adjust to the bright sunlight. He was about to head for Mary's place, when he saw, three straggly men, two went into the bank, while one waited with the horses.

He turned back towards the bar. Hey Gus, "Do you have any money in the bank?"

"Now that is being a little nosey Cole."

Well Gus "I was just wondering how much you were going to lose."

"What the hell are you talking about Cole?" Gus hollered.

Cole said; "I think your bank is getting robbed." Gus hurried to the door and looked outside, "All I see is a man on a horse." Then they heard a shot, from inside the bank.

Mary's eating house was three doors down from the bank, he saw Jenny come out and she was walking towards the bank. Cole went out the door. He moved towards the bank, almost at a run. He reached Jenny, one door from the bank, He grabbed her from behind and moved her into the alley, she was just about to scream, when Cole said; "I think the bank is going to be robbed." Her pretty blue eyes got very big and her mouth dropped open. "Do something she said;"

Cole smiled and said; "I just did, I got you out of harm's way." Then the shooting started, Cole saw the sheriff come out of the office and run towards the bank, pistol in hand, he fired a shot at the three men, not hitting anyone. One of the men fired back and the sheriff went down. Cole drew his colt and fired two quick shots, one man went down and another staggered but managed to get in the saddle and ride away.

The two men were shooting at anyone they saw, as they rode away. Cole told Jenny to stay where she was, running to the man that was down, covering him with his colt, Cole could see the man was dead, for he hit him dead center in the chest. By now, people were all over the street, some checking on the sheriff, who was, shot in the right shoulder. They helped the Sheriff to his feet. "Help me to my office and get the Doc," the sheriff Said. He looked at Cole, "Come with me will you?" In the Sheriff's office, he said to Cole, "looks like you got one." Cole said nothing. "I am going to need some help for a while, want a job asked the Sheriff."

Cole looked at the sheriff, "A little while ago, you wanted me out of town." The Sheriff smiled, "Things change, like the way you look at Jenny Mc Cloud, I think you want to stick around a while now."

John smiled, "For a lazy man, who sits around doing nothing all day, you don't miss much." The Sherriff just laughed. John shook his head, "I guess I better look this town over, and left the Jail."

─ CHAPTER 9 ─

THE SLATER'S

Sam and Joel Slater rode into Adobe Walls on two weary horses. The brothers were dirty and weary. They stopped at the first saloon they came to, dismounted, and tied their horses to the hitch rail, the bigger of the two looked around; he saw the Sheriff's office.

Sam turned to his brother, "A few drinks, and then I am going to kill Bill Cole."

Bill was looking out his office window, and saw the two walk into the saloon. He recognized them as Sam and Joel Slater. Sam was the gunfighter. He was always looking to make a bigger rep for himself. Joel was always trying to be like his brother. He was good with a gun, but not near as fast as his brother. Inside the saloon, Sam tossed his second drink down, then pulled his pistol, and shot a few shots into the big mirror over the bar. The few men in the saloon got out the door as fast as they could. Sam Slater turned and faced the twin bat doors. He punched the spent shells from his .44 colt, replacing them with new ones. Slater holstered his gun and adjusted the holster. "That should bring Cole out."

Then Sam heard Cole. "All right Slater come on out, let's get it over with."

The brothers walked out the door, Sam first. Sam stepped into the street, faced Cole, and without saying a word, went for his gun. His gun was just coming out of the tied down holster, when the bullet took him in the middle of the chest. He grunted and fell over backwards, his feet jerked a few times then stayed still. Joel looked at his brother, then at Bill Cole.

Bill holstered his gun, "If you want to be next to your brother then go for your gun." Joel shook his head; you killed my brother, I know you have a younger brother; I'm going to find him and kill him, like you did mine."

"Why don't you just go for your gun and get it over with."

"I am not going to draw on you Cole, I know I can't beat you, my brother was faster than me." He walked over to the hitch rail untied the reins and mounted his weary horse, pulled the horses head around to the left.

Bill drew his colt, "Keep both hands on the horn where I can see them Slater; do it right now or I will blow you out of the saddle." Slater put both of his hands on the horn, and looked at Cole with hateful eyes.

"Before you go, leave twenty in gold to bury your scum of a brother." Joel reached in his pocket and tossed Bill a double Eagle and kicked his horse into a trot. Bill watched him ride away, "You're a dead man Slater, you just don't know it yet", and Bill gave a small chuckle, and thought. "*If you go against my brother you are in for a hell of a surprise Slater, my brother John is faster than I am.*"

There were men all along the side of the street that watched the gunfight.

"One of you men, get the undertaker for me."

CHAPTER 10
PRACTICE

Cole looked at the Sheriff. "Sheriff I'm seventeen years old, I'm too young to be a lawman."

Pete looked at John, "I will tell you what to do, all I need is a right hand man until my shoulder heals, but in your case, a "left -hand man.""

The doctor stepped in the door; he was a very small man, with gray hair and glasses." "Let's see how bad it is Pete." John started for the door.

Pete groaned as the doctor looked at his shoulder, "Take the star Cole, it will impress Jenny, You get two dollars a day and can bunk here at the jail, save you hotel money. You will be rich in no time at all." John looked at the Sheriff, shook his head, picked up the badge, pinned it on and walked out the door. John thought what do I know about being a lawman? I am just a farm boy, whose brother taught him how to use a gun. Heading for the telegraph office, John thought, Bill is going to get a laugh out of this one. Bill asked the clerk, if there were any messages for him.

"One came in a while ago Mr. Cole."

STAY PUT (stop) WATCH OUT FOR SLATER (stop) GUNNING FOR YOU.

John sent a reply, OK (stop) I AM DEPUTY FOR NOW.

John left the telegraph office, and walked over to the stable and told Crenshaw, that the county would be paying him for the upkeep of his horse. As Cole left the stable, he heard Crenshaw mumble; I seen it all now, a kid acting deputy, a gunfighter at that. Maybe I should go in the undertaking business.

Cole shook his head and walked across the street back to hotel to collect his few belongings, after dropping them off at the jailhouse he headed towards Mary's for lunch. He wanted to see Jenny. As he walked down the street, he could see the people staring at him, as he passed a woman and a man, he tipped his hat. "I'm just helping the sheriff until his shoulder heals nothing permanent." Feeling self-conscious, he hurried to Mary's place. He opened the door, stood there waiting for his eyes to adjust to the dim light. He looked for a table close to the kitchen, where he could see Jenny better. When Jenny saw him, she smiled and walked over to him. "I want to thank you for the help this morning." John thought it was worth it just to get his arms around her.

"Oh, you are welcome, what is good, for lunch he asked?" Jenny smiled, "We have stew and dumplings or dumplings with stew, and apple pie." John returned the smile, "Well that is what I will have, with coffee." She turned and walked towards the kitchen; she looked back over her shoulder and saw John was looking at her. Thinking to herself, *I'm not the little girl with pigtails anymore, am I John.* After a short while, she brought him his food. Jenny turned to leave. Cole said; "Jenny would you have dinner with me some time"? With a smile she said "I would like that deputy." She then went to wait on other customers. John ate his food, drank his coffee, called his thanks to Jenny, and left the eating-place. As he stepped out the door, he waited for his eyes to adjust to the bright light. He thought he should go and see how the sheriff was doing. More stares as he walked to the sheriff's office. The sheriff was sitting in his chair, with a sling around his arm. "Sheriff did you recognize the man I killed?"

"Call me Pete. Yes, there is a wanted poster out on him and his brother .They are, or were the Dokes brothers, the one you killed was Clyde, the other one is Bart".

"Do you think I should go look for them"?

"Well John that would be the thing to do, but I am useless, so I need you here, and besides I am afraid that Bart will be back looking for you." "If he is the one you wounded, I do not think it will be too soon. But keep your eyes open."

John went to the back room, where he had dropped his meager belongings from the hotel. Thinking it would be a good time to give his horse some work and time for him to do some thinking. Taking up his saddlebags he walked out the door, into the bright afternoon sunshine. Walking to the stable, he got the same curious stares, when he got to the stable, he hollered, "Hey Crenshaw, can you bring my horse out here?" The old man led John's horse out of the barn. "You'll have to saddle her yourself."

John smiled and said; "I figured that", as he walked into the tack room, found his old worn saddle, carried it out, and saddled his horse and put his rifle in the boot. His hand on the horn, with the left rein tight, so the horse could not shy away as he mounted, walking Amber he headed out of town. At the outskirts of town, he let the mare trot for a time. Then knowing she wanted to run. He gave her, her head. Soon she was in a full gallop; he let her run for about a quarter of a mile, then slowed her down to a walk. Scanning the open prairie, he saw some lodgepole pines on top of a knoll. He headed Amber to the pines, dismounted, and thought this will do. He let the reins drag on the ground, knowing Amber would not go far. Opening his saddlebags, he took out an old worn holster and a box of .44 shells, strapped it on his right side. He picked out a skinny scrub tree, from the left side, in one fast and smooth movement he drew his gun and felt the gun buck in his hand three times. All shots hitting the now leaning tree. He punched out the spent shells and replaced them with new ones, then slid the colt into the right holster. Then in the same fast smooth draw, John fired three shots with his right hand missing with all three shots. Talking to himself, you got to remember, to aim a little to the right, allowing for the trigger pull. He tried again, hitting the tree with all three shots. If there was a difference between the left hand and right, it was so slim you could never tell. John practiced for about an hour, being satisfied; he whistled for Amber, she walked over to John and nuzzled him. John patted her neck then mounted and headed for town. From the top of the knoll, he could see the town. John talked to his horse Amber, as a lot of lonesome men do. "A nice town, but it will stay wild for a time yet." Thinking back, I am glad mom and dad made me use my right hand. You never know, when you might need the other hand. Ambidextrous, that's the word. That's how you got your name Amber old girl.

CHAPTER 11
DOKES

About thirty miles away, in a line shack, Bart Dokes, and a childhood friend called Carp, sat at a table with of bottle of whiskey. Carp asked; "How's the arm?"

"Just a flesh wound, in a few days it will be as good as new, and then we are going back to that town. I am going to kill that son of a bitch, who killed Clyde."

"I would be careful; He was very good with a gun."

"I did not say I was going to challenge him, I said I am going to kill him".

"How much money did we get?" Carp shook his head, "three hundred dollars I think, and Clyde had the larger bag with Gold coins." Bart asked; "Carp did you take care the horses?"

Hanging his head Carp said "well not yet." "Dam, Carp get out there and do it now, and then tomorrow I want you to go to town and watch things. Why do I put up with a stupid jerk like you? We need those horses."   Carp went out the door, mumbling to himself, as he went out and take care of the horses "He treats me like I'm stupid, it just takes me time to think."

While resting in the line shack, at the old broken table, waiting for his shoulder to heal, Bart thought of his now dead brother Clyde. Thinking back when they were young. The three of them had grown up somewhere on the Kansas prairie, How Carp came to live with them he could not remember. Carp being twelve years old, was one year younger than Bart. When Carp was young, a horse kicked him in the head. Since then Carp was never the same, he would always be slow in the head. After their mother died, their father Samuel started drinking heavily, on corn liquor he made himself. Sam was a mean drunk, and would beat on Bart all the time. One night for no reason, he beat on Bart, knocking him to the floor. Bart knew enough to stay on the floor until his Father fell asleep on the bed. Clyde and Carp huddled in fear in the corner of the small dirty cabin. When Bart heard his father snoring, he got up and told his Brother and Carp, not to worry, that Sam would not ever hit them again. Bart walked over to where his father had hung up his old pistol. Bart took the gun out of the old and worn leather holster. Walked over to the bed and pulled back the hammer on the gun, and put it against his father's head and pulled the trigger, ending his father's life. Bart felt no remorse for what he done; instead, he felt power and satisfaction. Bart liked the feeling. He would feel it many more times. The three lived there for five more years. Bart practiced every day with his father's gun. When he felt he was ready Bart told Clyde and Carp "Pack up, we are leaving." After a few years of robbing and killing, they rode into Abilene. As they rode down the rutted dusty street, Clyde looked the town over, seeing the Buffalo Saloon; he reined his horse in over to the hitching rail. As the three dismounted, Clyde saw the rickety bank a few doors down the street. That's when he decided to make himself some easy money.

CHAPTER 12
OLD ROCK

John rode back into town, pulled up in front of the Crenshaw's, dismounted and led Amber over to the watering trough, after the horse had his fill, John took the bridle and reins off Amber, grabbed a old burlap bag and rubbed him down, then put her in the corral, then walked over to the Sheriffs' office, and went inside.

The sheriff looked up at him. "We got a problem for you to take care. See the old man sitting in front of Clarks mercantile." John went to the window and looked out, "Ya I see him, looks real dangerous." "Pete said; well whenever he gets hungry enough, he does something to get thrown in jail, gives him a place to stay and eat. He just threw a rock threw Clarks window go drag him over here will ya."

John went out the door, walked across the street, stood in front of the old dirty man, who was sitting on the steps of the store. "Well deputy I done it take me to jail."

John said; "ok get up." The old man smiled, got up, and started heading for the jail. John grabbed him by the arm and dragged him over to the watering trough. He took him by the neck and stuck his head in the water holding him under for a bit. The old man came up coughing, "Why the hell you do that, if I was ten years younger I would beat the hell out of you."

"Hell, you're so dirty and stinky." John pushed all of him in the trough, he looked at the old man and said; "Stay there. Don't you move? Or you will get another dunking." John went into the mercantile; "Mr. Clark let me have a bar of soap." Clark gave him the soap.

"Who's going to pay for my window"?

"I will take care of it." John turned and went back out to the old man. Tossed the old man the soap, "Wash up good, clothes, and all. Or I will do it for you." John waited for the old man to finish. "Now you see that bucket over there. Get it and empty the trough. Then go around back to the pump and fill the trough back up, we don't want the horses to die, drinking all the grime that came off of you, then you can go clean up the broken glass at the store, and board up the window. When you are done, come over to the office."

"Then I will take you to get something to eat and buy you a beer."

The old man said; "And what if I won't do it?" John smiled and said; "Then you go to jail and all you will get is a piece of bread and water, every day until you change your mind." The old man looked at John "You will really buy me a beer?" John smiled and said; "Yes, I might even buy you two. Whenever you are that hungry come and see me, don't cause trouble. And you are going to work off the price of the window. What do they call you"? The old man smiled, and said; "They just call me Rock."

"Why just Rock?" The old man bent over and picked up a rock. "Don't you dare, I get it. Now get to work." The old man grumbled a bit, but said ; "ok", got the bucket, and started to empty the filthy water out of the trough before going around back to the pump. When John got back to the office, the sheriff asked; "well, where is our dangerous prisoner." John told him what he had done.

"See you will make a good lawman. Well it is getting late, I'm heading home, and my wife should have supper done. Hold down the fort, I will see you in the morning."

John sat down at the desk where he saw a bunch of wanted posters; he picked them up and started looking through them. When he came to Clyde Dokes poster, he took a pencil, and wrote Boot Hill. When he came to Bart's, he put it aside, and thought, I got to remember this face. John dozed in the chair for a while, when he woke, he looked out the window. The sun was just going down. He looked at Clarks mercantile. Rock had boarded up the mercantile widow. He smiled and said. "Well let's go feed the old man." John walked across the street to Clarks, where Rock was picking up the tools.

"Are you hungry Rock"? Rock looked at John with a scowl on his face; "Yep thirsty too." John laughed, "Looks like clean water in the trough."

"What about the beer you promised me"

"After we eat" Rock, give me a minute to talk to Mr. Clark, and then we will go over to Mary's and eat." The old man grumbled and sat down on the steps. John opened the door and said hello to Mr. Clark. "Well how is Rock doing?"

"Well deputy, I never would have believed it, but Rock is a good worker."

"Are you willing to let him work off the price of the window?"

"Yes and I told him he could work for me a few hours a day, if wants to make some money. He said he would like that."

John walked outside, "Sounds like you're doing good Rock, let's go eat."

As they entered Mary's place, the stage was just pulling in, Rock looked over his shoulder and saw a big man get off the stage. "Oh boy" said Rock, as they sat at a table.

"Oh boy what?" asked John

Looking out the window, Rock said; "You see that man heading for the Hotel, I saw him before, He's a professional fighter." John looked out the window towards the hotel, spotting the man Rock was talking about, "I don't know of any boxing matches planned for here."

Jenny walked over to their table, "Hi John, Rock, what will you have tonight."

"We will just have the special Jenny". John replied.

Rock looked at John. "Ya know Mr. Cole", Cole shook his head and stopped him, "Just call me John, you're old enough to be my father."

"Ok John, I was not always as I am now, when I was a young man in my twenties, I was married and had a son." John could see Rock's eyes starting to tear up.

"I was just starting my second year of medical school , when my wife and son came down with pox, the Doctors, nor I, could do anything to save them, they both died." That's when I decided, there's no use of me being a Doctor". "That's when I quit school, and started hitting the bottle, and headed west."

"Now don't tell anyone this, but Gus the bartender over at the saloon, he was not always a bartender, he was a prizefighter." They started calling him Gus the Killer, because he killed a man in the ring, after a few more fights, he quit fighting and disappeared." "The man that just got off the stage is the brother of the man Gus killed."

"Gus don't know it, but I saw him go fifteen rounds with, John L Sullivan, before Sullivan became champ, Gus is no man to fool with."

Mary brought them their food, "Thank you Ma'am, that sure looks tasty."

"You sure told me a lot today Rock. I am sorry for your loss, but you got to get your life together." "What's that man's name?"

"Craig Stone;" said Rock.

"I guess I will have to keep an eye on Mr. Stone." said John. The old man shook his head and warned.

"Don't ever let him hit you John; he could kill you with one punch."

"Don't worry Rock, he's twice my size, I won't fight him, with my fists, you know the old saying Rock." "God made man, but Sam Colt made all men equal."

They ate their meal and John called to Jenny. Jenny came over to the table, "How was the food"? She asked.

"Great as usual, can I stop by and have coffee with you later?"

Jenny smiled "That would be nice John."

As they got up from the table, "Would you like that beer now Rock?"

"That sounds real good to me". They walked out the door and headed for the saloon, as the last rays of the sun shown its light on the street.

They entered the saloon, and Rock headed towards the bar, John took his time and looked around the saloon. Stone sat at a table off to the side with a bottle of whiskey. John walked over to the bar and laid two bits on the bar. "Give us two beers, Gus." Gus brought the beers over and set them on the bar "Gus do you know that big man over there"? Asked John

"I know him; His brother was a boxer, remember I told you I killed a man once, it was his brother."

"Do you want me to stick around?"

"No need, he won't use a gun to get even, and I can take care of myself."

"Okay Gus, I will keep out of your business, but if you need me give a holler." John finished his beer, told Gus to give Rock a refill and left the saloon. It was getting close to the time for Mary's to close, so John went over and had coffee with Jenny before retiring for the night.

— CHAPTER 13 —

THE PUGILIST

Back at the bar, Stone got up from the table and walked over to the bar. "I have been looking for you a long time killer."

"Well now you found me."

Rock stood at the bar, listing to everything.

Stone stared at Gus. "Are we going to settle this someplace else or here?"

"A mile out of town, there is Millers creek with some pines around it we can settle it there; I would rather not get your blood all over my bar, your brother was a boxer same as me, he knew the risks, it was a fair fight."

"At ten tomorrow, it will be a fair fight also." Then Stone turned and left the Bar.

Rock finished his beer: "He's a lot younger than you Gus." Gus took the empty glasses from the bar and whipped the bar with a towel. "Yes he is and way over confident." Rock said good night and left the bar. The next morning, Gus walked over to Crenshaw's, "Cren, I need a horse for a few hours". Crenshaw pointed to a horse all ready saddled.

Gus shook his head. "Rock's been talking."

"You can't keep a secret in this town Gus." Gus mounted, and headed for Millers creek.

About thirty minutes later, Stone came to Crenshaw's stable. As usual

Crenshaw was sitting in his chair, just outside the stable door, having his second cup of coffee. Stone walked over to him; "Are you the owner?" Crenshaw was about to give the man a smart answer, like he always did, but the size of the man, changed his mind.

"Yes sir; what can I do for you?"

"I would like to buy a horse and saddle."

Crenshaw looked the man up and down.

Stone looked hard at Crenshaw; "Is there a problem."

"Nope none at all, I only have one horse left that is big enough to carry a man your size."

Stone looked around, "That big red roan looks strong enough."

Crenshaw said "The roan is for sale, Seventy- five dollars, comes with, saddle, blanket and bridle."

"Are you trying to rob me old man?"

"Nope take it or leave it, don't matter to me."

Stone gave him a dirty look, reached in his pocket and took out a bunch of green backs, and peeled of seventy-five dollars and gave the money to Crenshaw. Crenshaw took the money stuffed it in his pocket; "Gear is just inside the door."

"Stone saddled the red roan. "Where is Millers creek?"

Crenshaw pointed towards the west, "That way a mile or so." Stone Mounted and headed in the direction, Crenshaw had pointed. As soon as he had left; Crenshaw closed up the stable doors, walked over to his old mule, mounted and headed for Millers Creek too.

When Gus reached Millers Creek, he stopped and looked around; there must have been twenty men there waiting. Gus dismounted, and someone took his horse for him.

Twenty minutes later Stone rode up and dismounted someone took his horse "Don't go too far with her, this won't take long."

Stone walked over to Gus. "One rule Killer, there aren't' any."

"Suit yourself: Stone."

Both men took off their coats and shirts. Rock hollered, "I got two dollars on Gus." And so the betting started.

The two men approached each other, without warning, Stone threw a left jab at Gus, he saw it coming and moved his head to the left, but was hit a glancing blow, to the side of his face. Gus countered with a right, but missed. It had been ten years since Gus had been in a fight; there is a big difference between thirty and forty years old. The brain still knew what to do but the body reacts slower. Both men stood toe-to-toe, trading punches; Gus was receiving more punches than he gave. Stone, hit him with a left jab then a hard right to the jaw, driving him back, he staggered and almost went down. Stone did not follow through, for he wanted to punish Gus.

"What's wrong killer, not so good anymore?" he taunted.

Gus answered with a jab to stone's face and a right to Stones belly, driving Stone back towards the crowd. Stone threw a hard right at Gus's face; Gus ducked and hit Stone with a hard right to the body. Stone was losing his cockiness; he blocked the next two punches thrown at him, and hit Gus in the nose with a left jab and followed with a right to the face. Gus countered with another right to Stone's belly; Stone was feeling the effect of the punches to the body. Gus noticed whenever he hit Stone in the belly, Stone would drop his right arm down to block the blow. Gus faked a right to the belly, Stone dropped his right arm down to block the punch; Gus threw a hard left hook to the jaw, then a hard right to the face, then followed with another left and a right. Stone went down and did not move. Stone was out cold. The men were slapping the bartender on the back and hooting, way to go Gus. He heard Rock; "Pay up Clark."

Gus said; "Some of you men to put Stone on his horse and take him to the Doc." He put on his shirt and coat, and then mounted his horse. "I got a bar to run." and rode back to town, he knew business would be good today.

CHAPTER 14
FAREWELL
ADOBE WALLS

Bill Cole sat at his desk going over paper work. In walked the Mayor. Bill looked up, "Morning Caleb", knowing something was not going to be good. Morning visits from the Mayor; were never social calls.

"Good morning; Bill, This is not going to be easy for me."

Bill leaned back in his chair, "Just spit it out."

"Well at the town meeting the other night, the board was not happy, with the shoot out the other day. Your reputation keeps bringing gunfighters here. They want you to resign Bill." Bill got up from his chair and faced the Mayor with an angry look on his face.

"When I took this job, you agreed I could have it as long as I wanted it. Now that I got rid of the riff raff, you want me out. You know, I did not get rich on the lousy thirty dollars a month you pay me."

The Mayor said; "The board voted to give you two months pay, Bill it is out of my hands. They want to have a police force; they do not want just one man. They are hoping it will not attract gunfighters looking for a big reputation." Bill shook his head.

"Have my money in the morning; I want it in gold not greenbacks. I want the black Stallion with a bill of sale. Until tomorrow, this is my office; Get the hell out."

That evening Bill started gathering his things. He did not want to stay in this town any longer than he had to. After packing, he walked out the door, heading for the stable, passing a few men on the way.

"Evening Sheriff."

"Not for long," Bill said and walked on.

The evening was cool and cloudy. Bill looked at the sky, yep rain in the morning, just what I need.

Smitty was standing in front of the stable. "I heard what they done Bill. I think it is a big mistake."

"Thanks Smitty, you are the only friend I have in this lousy town." Bill asked Smitty; "If you could have the Black ready for me in the morning, I would appreciate it."

"No problem Bill, He'll be ready."

Bill turned and walked to the saloon. As he entered, the men turned and looked at him. He walked to the bar; men moved aside and made room for him.

He laid a nickel on the bar, "Beer". The bartender poured him a warm beer, pushed the nickel back at Bill.

"You drink on the house tonight Bill, I don't like what they are doing to you. You made this town a better place to live." Behind him, two men were facing each other and arguing, hands close to their guns. Bill turned around looked at the two men.

"Take it out in the street, I don't want to get hit by a stray bullet, my last night in this town." The two men turned and walked out the door. After a few minutes, two shots rang out. Bill unpinned his badge laid it on the bar. Not my problem let the new police take care of it. Bill drank his beer, the bartender poured him another.

In the morning, Bill woke up with a hangover. He did not have to get dressed for he fell asleep in his clothes, boots, and all. Bill got his saddlebags and bedroll. He laid the keys to the office on the desk, picked up a stack of wanted posters and walked out the door. Looking up at the cloudy sky Bill muttered "Even the weather is against me." He walked over to the cafe where he wolfed down breakfast. Bill put two bits on the table and went out the door over to the Mayor's office. Bill collected his money and the bill of sale for the big black horse. Not saying a word he went out the door to the stable. Smitty was there with the black ready to go. Bill shook hands with Smitty.

"See ya around sometime Smitty."

"Good luck Bill." As Bill mounted the big Black he thought to himself; now where was it John is at?

Bill rode out of Adobe Walls heading for Kansas, across the Llano Estacado; it would be a long and boring ride, for the Stalked Plains were miles and miles of nothing. Time was not a big factor. He was hoping he could pick up some bounty money on the way. About a week out on the plains, Bill noticed a dust cloud, about two miles behind him. He was not too concerned with Indians, for most of the Indian troubles were over, but there were still some out on the plains, and a lone rider was hard to turn down, for guns and horses were still hard to come by. He knew where the water holes were, and he knew he could reach one before nightfall. Bill put the big black into a trot, wanting to keep ahead of the men following him. Upon reaching the watering hole, he dismounted and took out his field glasses, looking back about a mile he could make out enough to see it was three Indians following him. There was no place to hide on the flat Stalked Plains. He put the glasses back in his saddlebag and took his Winchester from the scabbard and laid it on the ground. He unsaddled the big black and ground hitched him near the water hole. Knowing they would reach him before dark, he looked around for a Buffalo hollow, finding one about thirty yards from the water hole, he laid his saddle on the top of the hollow and laid down in the smelly dirt, where buffalo had pissed and rolled in it to keep the lice off. With the Winchester across the saddle he waited, knowing they would be upon him very soon.

When the Indians were about three hundred yards away they spread out and kicked their horses into a gallop, screaming as they came. At about two hundred yards Bill drew a bead on the bay horse to the far left, for the man was too small of a target. He hated to kill the horse, but his life was at stake. Bill pulled back the hammer of the Winchester, took a deep breath and slowly squeezed the trigger; he felt the kick of the rifle and saw the horse go down. Now only a hundred yards separated them. He levered a shell into the rifle and drew a bead on the Indian on the big black horse and fired. The Indian flipped over the back of the horse, not having time to get another shell into the rifle, Bill dropped the rifle and rolled over too his right, just as an arrow went into the dirt where he was laying. Coming up on his knees he drew his colt and put two shots in the last Indian. The Indian slid off the horse to the ground, with the reins wrapped around his hand; the horse dragged him for about ten yards then stopped. Bill opened the gate on his pistol, ejected the spent shells and quickly replaced them with new ones. Closing the gate he spun the cylinder to be sure it was okay, Then walked over to the closest Indian, there was no doubt he was dead. He untangled the rein from the dead Indians hand and led the fine looking Appaloosa to the watering hole, where he ground hitched him. Then went and checked on the other two Indians, both were dead. Bill looked for the big black. The black was standing about fifty yards away, as Bill walked towards him, he stamped the ground and shook his head and backed away. Talking out loud to the horse, "You're going to give me a hard time I can tell, but you're a good looking stallion and I'm not going to lose you, you're not going to go too far from the mare or the water, I can wait." He walked over to the water hole and made camp for the night. Sitting by the fire with a cup of Coffee in his hand, and the rope next to him he waited. The fire cast just enough light for Bill to see the mare. Bill thought they will make a good pair for breeding.

After a while the mare whinnied, the Stallion answered, Bill set down his cup, picked up the rope, and slowly got to his feet.

The Stallion slowly moved over to the Mare, with one turn of the rope over his head, and a flick of his hand, the rope sailed over the Stallion's head. Bill braced his feet on the ground expecting the Stallion to put up a fight. The horse gave a pull, but the stallion had a rope on him before and did not try to get away. Bill coiled the rope as he moved towards the stallion, talking as he walked; when he reached the horse he rubbed its ears. he took the short piece of rope and keeping his eyes on the horse he bent down and tied the rope around the horses two front feet, leaving enough room for the horse to walk, but not enough to run. The stallion tried to bite him as he was tying the rope; a small smack on the nose stopped the horse from biting him. Bill reached out and scratched the horse between his ears, "if we are going to get along, you will have to learn not to bite me". Bill noticed the double C brand on both horses. He walked back to his fire and finished his cup of coffee. Talking to out loud to himself "Looks like we got a good start on our horse ranch."

Bill broke camp and headed for Abilene, leading the two horses behind him. Thinking this is better than any bounty money, with

Any luck he could find the double C brand owner, and make some kind of deal.

CHAPTER 15

REUNION

After so many days on the trail, Bill was weary and so were the horses, as he entered the town, he looked for the stable, not seeing one he asked a man sitting on the porch in front of the Mercantile? "Keep going down the street, at the first street you comes to hang a left. Sign will say Crenshaw's." Bill tipped his hat and rode at a slow walk down the dusty road.

Bill dismounted, in front of the barn. Crenshaw stepped out the door. "That will be Two bits a day per horse." Bill took off his hat and knocked the dust off it. He reached in his pocket, and tosses the old man five silver dollars "I will be here a while, keep the blacks apart, the one without the blaze is a mean one. Then he walked across the street to the Saloon.

Crenshaw looks at the tied down Gun. "Yep, I should go into the undertaking business." Bill pushes in the bat wing doors and waits for his eyes to adjust to the dim Smokey room. He walked over to the bar "Beer, cold if you have it."

Gus looks Bill over. "That will be a nickel; we only have cold beer in the winter."

"I am looking for John Cole; you know where I can find him.

Gus looked at Bill; "I won't stand for any trouble in here."

Gus was a big man, he stood over six feet tall and weighed over two hundred pounds, and had huge hands. Rock was swamping the bar; he stopped and looked at Gus. Gus nodded. Rock set his mop down and hurried out the door running to the Sheriff's office where he entered out of breath."

"Deputy there is a man at Gus's Saloon asking for you, he wears his gun low and tied down, like a gunfighter."

John looks at the sheriff, "Sure you want me as a deputy? It looks like trouble is going to always find me."

John headed for the door and walked over to the Saloon. He pushed the door open and waited for his eyes to adjust to the dim light.

As John steps into the saloon he asks, "Who's looking for me?" Men at the table got up and got back against the wall. Bill turns around and says.

"That would be me." John smiled and walks over to Bill. He reached out his hand.

"Good to see you brother, let's, sit at a table and have a beer, and catch up." John put two nickels on the bar. Gus poured two beers. They picked up their beers and sat at a table facing the door. They could hear men whispering. That's Bill Cole; the gunfighter. The brothers paid no attention to them.

John asked; "What are you doing here?" Bill explained what happened.   Then he asked, "What's that badge doing on your chest."

"No big deal, it's only temporary." He told about the shoot out. Bill told him he knew the Dokes brothers, "You should have killed Bart, he's the worst of the two." John laughed; "Next time I will ask who's the worse "Are you hungry?"

"I could use a bite."

"Well lets go over to Mary's café, There is a girl named Jenny I want you to meet, I kind of like her, so don't get any ideas." They drank their beer, pushed the chairs back and walked out the door. Both waited, for their eyes to adjust, to the light. As the two brothers walked down the dusty street, John told his brother; "You can bunk at the Jail, I use a small room in the back. Nobody is in the two cells, so you can bunk in one."

John entered Mary's place. Bill was right behind him. The place was crowded for it was noontime. Bill looked around and saw a young pretty girl waiting on tables. Now he could see why his brother was taken with her. Jenny saw John, and motioned him over to the table close to the kitchen. As they sat down, facing the door. John said; "Hi Jenny, this is my brother Bill." With a smile; that would melt any man, Jenny said: "Nice to meet you Bill."

She took their order and walked to the kitchen. John noticed Bill's eyes following her. John cleared his throat, looking at Bill.

"Well you can't blame a guy for looking, she's a sight."

John smiled; "as long as you only look." Bill and John finished eating. Bill said, "Did you sell everything?"

John shook his head, "No I just sold the corn harvest and what hay I got from the high field, I was going to ask Mr. Martin down at the bank to see if he could sell the property for us and hold the money in the bank."

"But a young couple, name of Johnson, with a daughter and young boy stopped by the farm. They had a broken down wagon and a worn out mule, and looked like they had not eaten in a while."

"They asked if they could rest there for a while. I told them they could, we introduced ourselves to each other, and I asked them to have dinner with me."

"Mr. Johnson said they were not looking for charity. I told him I was tired of eating my own cooking and if his wife and daughter would do the cooking, it would make me happy."

He said in that case, they would accept."

"His wife made a great meal, ham, potatoes and corn. "I told Mr. Johnson that I planned on heading west for a while to see you, and would like to make some kind of a deal with him, I told him that I did not want to sell the place, and was thinking maybe he could homestead it for me till I came back, I told him he could use what you need to feed his family, and any profit that was made we could split. He said he could never find a better offer, and he would be a fool not to except. We shook on it and he said he would do his best to make it a better place or as good as it was now."

Bill said; "Sounds good to me, do you plan on going back?" John said; "I didn't think about it till I met Jenny, Their daughter Amy looked pretty good, maybe you should come back with me, "The property belongs to both of us."

After they finished their coffee, they pushed back their chairs. John took four bits from his pocket and laid them on the table.

John said; "I will meet you outside in a minute."

He waited for Jenny to walk over to him.

"Jenny, tomorrow is Sunday, would you go on a picnic with me?"

Jenny smiled and said; I think mom will give me some time off, there is a nice grove down near Millers Creek, I will pack us a lunch."

John asked; "If eight would be ok?" Jenny smiled and said;

"That would be fine."

"See you then Jenny."

John walked over to the door and stepped outside. He looked at his brother, "You're on your own tomorrow, I got plans".

"Gee now what could they be." As they walked over to the jail, Bill said; "There is something familiar, about that girl."

"I been thinking the same thing."

John and Bill walked down the street to the Jail.

When they entered, Sheriff Murphy was sitting with his feet on the desk, looking at John with questing eyes. "This is my brother Bill". Murphy stuck out his hand; Bill shook his hand, "Nice to meet you sheriff."

"I told Bill he could bunk with me if that's ok with you."

Pete said, "I see no problem with that, last I heard you were Sheriff somewhere over in Texas."

Bill smiled, "That's right sheriff, dangers and the pay was terrible, going to do some bounty hunting. I'd like to check the wanted posters later."

Pete shook his head, "Glad to see your taking up a safe job now."

Bill laughed, "A man got to make a living."

━ CHAPTER 16 ━
PIGTAIL

John woke before the sun was up. Went to the woodbin, got some kindling and started a small fire. Then he went out back to the pump, washed his face and filled the coffee pot and a pail with water, looked to the east across the flat open land. John could just see rays of light on the horizon. John said to himself, this should be a fine day for our picnic. He went back inside the office and put the coffee pot on the stove. Then he went in the back to his room, picked up his saddlebag, set it on the chair next to the table. John took out his soap mug, razor, and small mirror; the mirror had a crack in it. Soaped his face and shaved the slight boyish whiskers from his face. He knew he did not really need a shave, but he wanted to look good for Jenny. John took out the only other shirt he had from his saddlebag and put it on. He then walked over to the stove, the water was boiling, and He took a handful of coffee and put it in the boiling water. After the coffee boiled for about five minutes, he poured himself a cup, sat in the chair and waited for the sun to rise. John sat for what seemed like hours, but was only about thirty minutes; He could sit no longer, got up and put his gun on, and went out the door.

Trying to kill time, he walked over to the stable, banged on the small side door, and hollered "Crenshaw". The door opened, and Crenshaw "Said what ya want so early Cole."

John smiled; "I am going to need a buggy about nine thirty".

The old man shook his head "You got to tell me now, what ya think it will take me three hours to get it ready."

"Well old man, the way you move it just might" John gave a chuckle. Crenshaw smiled and said; "You better move on sonny, or I will have to take you over my knee and spank you." John made as if he was scared and hurried away.

"Well I think I will see if Gus got the coffee ready." John walked across the street to the saloon. John looked down the street to Mary's place. There were a lot of people were going in, including Rock. Rock saw John and waved, then went in for breakfast.

John stepped into the empty saloon looked around and saw no one. "Hey Gus are you around?"

Gus came in from a back room; "What's up Cole?"

"I thought maybe I could get a cup of coffee off of you."

Gus went back into the back room then came back out with a coffee pot and two cups, place them on the bar, and poured them both a cup of coffee.

"What brings you in so early Cole?"

"I think you know me well enough to call me John."

"Well Gus I am taking Jenny for a picnic today and got some time to kill." John no sooner got the cup to his mouth when Rock came in, all out of breath. "John there is a man at the café giving Jenny a hard time." John dropped the cup on the bar and moved out the door and down the street as fast as he could. John saw red when he saw the man with his arms around Jenny and her trying to get away. John hurried over to the man, whipped out his gun; put the barrel against the man's head.

"Let her go or I will blow your head off."

The man let go and looked at John, "I was not going to hurt her, I just wanted a little kiss."

John grabbed him by the shirt and dragged him out the door to the jail. John threw the man in a cell and locked the door.

The man saw Bill lying on the cot, "Hey the man in the other cell has a gun."

Bill rolled over, looked at the man, "Ya and if you don't shut up, I am going to shoot you with it." The man shut up and sat on the cot. Bill got up opened the cell door and walked over to the stove, and got a cup of coffee.

"What did this one do brother?" John was still mad," he tried getting too friendly with Jenny."

Bill looked at the man in the cell," "It is a bad thing to mess with the deputy's girl" and laughed."

John looked at Bill; "I don't think its funny brother

He's lucky I did not bust his head."Then he walked out the door and walked around town killing time, until it was time to pick up Jenny.

When John went out the door, it hit Bill; he laughed and said out loud, "Pigtail."

The man in the cell looked at Bill and thought he was crazy, but was too scared to say anything.

— CHAPTER 17 —
SLATER ARRIVES

Joel Slater never left Adobe Walls; he camped outside of town near a small grove next to a small creek. He thought long and hard about shooting Bill Cole in the back,

But after finding out that Bill was no longer going to be sheriff, of Adobe Walls. He figured Bill might lead him to John. Sure enough, he saw Bill Leaving Adobe Walls, and trailed him at a safe distance. After days on the trail, he knew where Bill was going. Joel thought again of trying to get closer to Bill and back shoot him. Being the coward that he was, Joel gave up that Idea, and decided to just go into Abilene and wait for a chance at John. Joel Slater rode into Abilene. He looked up and down the dusty streets, making sure not to let Bill Cole see him. As Slater rode down the street, he saw a man and woman were heading out of town. Not wanting to draw any attention to himself, and being as polite as he could.

"Sir, could you direct me to the stable?"

The Man slowed the buggy down, "At the first intersection take a left you won't miss it."

Joel slowly rode down the street, keeping his head down, turned at the crossroad saw the stable and headed for it. Old man Crenshaw was sitting out front drinking his morning coffee. Joel dismounted, "I would like to board my horse for a few days."

Crenshaw nodded "Two bits a day." Joel reached into his pocket, pulled out a silver dollar and flipped it to Crenshaw,

"I will be here a few days, "Who's the law in this town Mr.?" "Crenshaw's the name; well Pete Murphy is the Sheriff, and John Cole is acting as his deputy." Joel nodded and looked around and saw the hotel, took his saddle roll of the back of his horse, then pulled his rifle out of the boot and walked to the hotel, looking, around making sure that Bill was not around.

He entered the hotel walked over to the desk,

"I would like a room for a few days facing the street."

The clerk said, "Two bits a day." Joel gave him a dollar and walked up the stairs to his room. After entering the room, Joel laid his gear on the floor, pulled up a chair next to the window, and watched the street. Joel slept in the chair all night. When he awoke, he saw John picking up Jenny. Joel noticed the blanket and picnic Basket. He thought maybe he would follow and have it out with John Cole. Thinking to his self, no I want his brother to see me kill him. Hours later he saw the buggy, riding fast, pull in front of the doctor's office. He watched as they helped John quickly off the buggy and into the Doc's. Noticing the hand being bandaged, he looked at the tied down gun on the left, the same as the injured hand.

He laughed and said aloud, "This is getting better all the time." Joel Slater kept out of site as much as he could. He ate his meals late at night, just watching for the Cole brothers. The next day, at noontime he saw Bill and John; go into Mary's place. He got up from the chair, strapped on his Gun walked down the stairs and out the door of the Hotel. Joel looked all around the street, He walked over to Mary's place, and he stood to the left of the door out of sight and waited.

CHAPTER 18
THE PICNIC

John walked down the street to Crenshaw's stable. The old man was waiting for him with the buggy. As John got close, Crenshaw smiled. "Well lookey here, all cleaned up."

"Don't start on me old man". As John got up into the buggy, he saw Crenshaw staring at him.

"Ok what you staring at?"

Crenshaw laughed, "I was just trying to see the love bite, Har, Har." John shook his head and slapped the rein on the horses back," get up". John pulled the buggy up when he got to Mary's place.

Jenny was standing on the front porch," Good morning John." John stepped down, and took the blanket and picnic basket from Jenny and placed it in the back of the buggy.

Then he helped Jenny up on the seat, said "Good morning Jenny." John walked around the horse and climbed up into the Buggy. John looked at Jenny and smiled, thinking she sure is pretty. "What way to miller's creek Jenny, I never had been there?" Jenny told him to just head out of town the way we are headed. They rode out of town about a mile or so;

"You see the stand of cotton woods over there." John said he did and headed for the trees. At the top of the knoll, John saw the small creek running amongst the trees, along the creek next to the trees was a large patch of green grass. John pulled the buggy close to the trees, so the horse would be in the shade; he set the brake, got down and helped Jenny down.

Jenny took a blanket and picnic basket out of the back of the buggy, and spread it down on the lush grass. John not having had much to do with woman was having a hard time letting Jenny know how he felt. John cleared his throat, "Jenny I have a small farm in Ohio, and am thinking of going back to it."

Being coy, Jenny said; "Oh I will miss you John." John stammered, "I was hoping you would come back with me."

Jenny opened the picnic basket, took out two plates, put some friend Chicken, boiled potatoes and bread on them.

Jenny looked at John, "Are you asking me to marry you John?"

"Well yes I am."

"I could not leave my mother here all alone."

"Your mom could come with us."

"John there are a few things you need to know first, I would have to talk to mom. And, also there is the gun; I don't want a husband that I have to worry about all the time."

"Jen, Ohio is not like it is here; it is not as wild so I won't need to wear a gun."

Jenny smiled; "Well there is one more thing, but it will keep for now." They ate there food and chatted about things he would like to do on the farm, and the people who were share cropping the place. The time flew bye, and it was time to return. Jenny had to help with the evening meal.

John said he would wash the dishes. John picked up the dishes walked down to the creek and started washing the dishes. When one dish was clean, he reached out with his left hand and put the dish on a rock. Too late, he heard the rattle; the snake struck and bit him on the back of his left hand, he pulled back as the rattler was ready to strike again, he reached across his body, drew his pistol with his right hand and blew the snakes head off. Jenny jumped up and ran over to John; she saw the snake and knew what happened. John took out his penknife, made two slits where the puncture wounds were and sucked out as much blood and venom as he could. Jenny looked at John's finger, "Oh John it is swelling already, we have to get to town and have the Doc look at it." Hurrying to the buggy,

John started to get a little dizzy; His hand felt like his blood was on fire as red hot shots of burning pain ran up his arm. Jenny helped him up on to the buggy, then got up beside him, released the break, turned the horse towards town, and drove as fast as she could. As she came into town, Old man Crenshaw saw her pull in front of the Doctors office; He hurried over and helped her get John down from the wagon.

"Snake bite", she told Crenshaw, as they got John into the office. They had to help hold him up for he was very dizzy. Carefully they placed John in a chair. Doctor Shaw looked at the hand.

"Well he is lucky, the bite did not hit any big veins, all we can do is clean the wound and try to keep the fever down."

Rock, who always seemed to know what is going on went to the sheriff's office and got Bill. Bill hurried over to the Doc's office and helped carry John over to the sheriff's office. They put John on the cot in the back room, where he was to stay quiet and rest for twenty-four hours. Bill told Jenny and Crenshaw that they could go.

"I am staying with him till he is ok," said Jenny.

Jenny filled a bowl with cool water sat in a chair and bathed Johns hot feverish face. Jenny stayed all night and by morning John's fever was down, but his left hand was hurting and very badly swollen. When she knew John was out of danger, Jenny went home to the café.

John was awake and feeling better, he got up from the bunk and walked into the office. Bill looked at him and asked "How are you feeling brother?"

"Except for the hand I feel good, and I am hungry."

"That's a good sign John; now let's get something to eat." John reached for his gun belt.

"You won't need the gun John; I talked to the Sheriff about helping out until your hand is better." The two brothers went out the door and headed for Mary's place. Bill told John how Jenny stayed with him all night, until his fever was gone. As they walked down the dusty street to Mary's place, John told his brother, "I asked Jenny to marry me."

"That is no surprise I saw it coming, what was her answer?"

"I am not sure yet, she does not want to marry someone she has to worry about."

They entered Mary's and sat at a table, John looked around for Jenny.

An old Mexican lady who helped out at times came out of the kitchen, walked over to the table.

John asked? "Where is Jenny?"

She smiled, "Senor, she was up all night with you, do you think she no needs sleep?" She took their order and walked into the kitchen. A short while later she brought out their food and a pot of coffee. The brothers talked as they ate.

Bill told John "When your hand is better I will be leaving, the money I have won't last forever."

"What will you do for a living?"

"I have been a law man for a long time and have nothing to show for it, there is good money in bounty hunting, if I'm lucky I can make some good money, when I save enough, I would like to go back to the farm and hang up the gun."

"I want to go back also if Jenny will marry me; maybe together we can raise some horses and make a go of it."

"Well John, we fulfilled our dreams and became gunfighters; it's just not as exciting as we thought it would be, we never once thought that we could get killed. But that's the dreams of boys, nothing like it really is."

"I know sometimes I wish I'd never left the farm, but then I never would have met Jenny." Bill gave a small chuckle. "What's so funny?"

"You will find out, when the time is right." John just shook his head, "If you say so."

They finished the lunch, John left the money on the table and they walked out the door.

Joel Slater was standing behind them on the sidewalk with his gun drawn. "Hold it right there both of you, and keep your hand away from your gun Bill. Unbuckle your gun belt with your left hand and let it fall on the ground" Joel turned to John and said' "Your brother killed mine, now I'm going to kill you."

Bill said; "If you shoot us in the back they will hang you Slater."

"I'm not going to shoot you in the back; this will be a fair fight, now step away from the gun and keep your back to me." Joel bent down and took the pistol from the holster and said; 'Ok Bill pick up the holster and put it on your brother." Bill picked up the holster, "You call this a fair fight, knowing he can't use his Gun hand."

Joel said; "Just put it on him."

John said; "Put on low and tie it down."

Joel said; "Ok turn around."

As John was turning he said; "I know you're not too bright Slater; did you ever hear the word ambidextrous?"

Joel said; "nope, and don't care , I am going to back out into the street, when I get there, pick up your brothers gun with your bad hand and put it in your holster."

John bent down, picked up the gun with his injured hand.

"Ok deputy, walk out and meet me, I want everyone to see me kill you in a fair fight."

John looked up and saw the sun at Slater's back as he walked out into the street, he walked to the right, so the sun would not be in his eyes and faced Slater, looking into Slater's eyes, like Bill had told him. Some men can tell when another is going to draw by their eyes. "Make your move Slater."

John knew the moment Slater would go for his gun, in one quick movement John drew and fired.

Slater's hand was just on the butt of his pistol, instantly he felt something smash into his chest. He looked down and saw the blood pumping out of his chest. He looked at John, with

disbelieving eyes. Then Joel Slater fell over backwards, and the last thing he heard was, "It means either hand."

Bill said; "I forgot mom and dad had to always tell you to use your right hand."

Joel said; "Ya good for me, bad for Slater."

~ CHAPTER 19 ~
PROPOSAL ACCEPTED

Jenny heard the shot, got up and went to the dining room, "Mom I heard a shot, has John been in?" "Mary said: "He just went out a few moments ago." Jenny hurried and went out the door; she saw John and Bill standing over a man in the street. "Oh! Not again John." John turned and walked over to Jenny. "I had no choice Jenny, he has been looking for me for awhile, but it is over now."

"John it will never be over, it will always be the gun and I will always be scared that it will be you lying in the street. I don't know if I can live like that."

John turned to Bill, unhooked the gun belt and handed it to him. "Bill I will see you later, I am going to have a talk with Jenny." "Jen lets go and talk over a cup of coffee." She nodded and turned and walked back into the café; John followed, She walked into the kitchen and quickly returned with two cups of coffee, she sat down at the table with him and looked at him waiting. John reached across the table and took her hand. "Jenny a man could get killed even if he doesn't wear a gun, you could have been killed the day the bank got robbed."

"I know, but I will always worry."

"Jen in about another month Sheriff Murphy will be all healed, and then we can get married, and leave for Ohio". "I can't say I will never need a gun, for the west is a dangerous place, but Ohio is not like it is here."

"John I know what Ohio is like, I use to live there." John looked at her with a confused look. Jenny smiled, "I guess you should know something."

"Ok tell me what it is."

"I was going to tell you before we got married, not that it should matter, well I hope it won't, my name was not always Mc Cloud, My father died and mom got married again. I was young so I used the new name". It uses to be Jenny Walker."

John's mouth dropped open! "Pigtail!"

"Yea, does it make a difference?"

John stuttered, "Of course not, but it was Bill you always followed around, not me."

"No John it was always you, you just never thought of girls back then."

John got hold of himself. "Kind of funny how things happen. Back then I never would have dreamed I would ask you to marry me, but who would have guessed you would turn out so beautiful."

'Why thank you John, I think."

"Well Jen, you were a skinny runt, not to mention a pain in the neck." John laughed; "What's your answer, are you going to marry me?"

"Yes, as long as you don't wear a badge and only wear a gun when you have too." John leaned across the table, and gave her a kiss, "I promise."

John entered the sheriffs' office. Pete Murphy was sitting at the desk. "Pete, your arm looks like it is healing, I will help you for only a few more weeks then I am going home, with Jenny and her mom. I'm going to make my rounds, get something to eat then turn in for the night." Pete nodded and John walked out the door. Thinking to himself, I sure hope this will be a nice quiet night. John walked up one side of the street and down the other, checking all the stores, making sure they were locked. Then he headed for the bar for a beer.

CHAPTER 20
TRACKING DOKES

Two weeks after the shoot out with Joel Slater, Bill Cole said goodbye to his brother and the friends he had made in Abilene. Bill told John that after he made some money he would head back to the Ohio Farm and would wire him from time to time, to let him know where he was, and hoped he would see John back at the farm. Bill asked his brother all about the bank robbery, John told him about it, and that the sheriff said they were the Dokes brothers, and another man. Bill asked if there was a bounty on them. John told him," The sheriff said the bank manager told him he would pay for Bart Dokes dead or alive." Before leaving town Bill decided to have a beer at the saloon. Bill had his horse and gear all ready to leave; he walked his horse over to the saloon, tied him to the hitching rail and entered the saloon. Bill pushed the double bat wing doors open stepped inside and waited for his eyes to adjust to the dim light in the saloon. He looked around the saloon it was almost empty. There were a few men at a table having a beer, and a big man sitting alone with his head down, Rock was sweeping up the place. Bill walked over to the bar, said hello to Gus. He laid a nickel on the bar and said "Beer Gus" Gus said hello and poured him a beer, taking a flat stick and wiping the foam off the top of the glass. "Gus, do you remember anything about the bank robbery that could help me find them." Gus shook his head, "All I saw was big man holding the horses, there was something strange about him but I can't remember what it was." Gus looked at the man sitting alone then it hit him. Bill, "Now I remember. The man that held the horses had his shirt inside out."Then Gus nodded at the big man at the table. The man at the table had his shirt inside out. Bill said; "Don't pay any attention to him, maybe he will lead me to the one who got away."

After a while Carp got nervous and got up without looking at anyone and left the saloon. Bill walked over to the door and watched the way Carp went. Bill then went out of the saloon, untied his horse from the hitching rail, mounted and followed Carp.

Carp was scared so he hurried back to where Bart was hiding out. It was almost dark when Carp reached the old-line shack. He dismounted dropped the reins on the ground and hurried into the shack. Bart had his pistol out and almost shot Carp.

Bart cursed and hollered, "You stupid idiot, don't you know enough not to burst in like that, now what the hell is the big hurry?"

Shaken Carp said; "I think they knew who I was."

Bart swore, "Who is they, and did they follow you here?"

Carp mumbled "The bartender and the brother of the kid who shot Clyde, I did not see anyone following me."

Bart cursed, "If anyone followed you here I will shoot you myself, now get out there, and keep your eyes open."

Bill watched Carp enter the shack, then rode around behind it, and stopped in a gully, where he could not be seen. The prairie, though it looks flat, has a lot of gullies and hills. Bill tied his horse to a scrub bush and crawled to the top of the gully, where he could watch the shack and not be seen. Bill saw Carp sitting on the porch, with a rifle in his hand looking all around. Bill slowly made his way to the side of the building took off his hat and looked around the corner. Bill could hear Carp mumbling to himself, "He always makes me do the dirty work, I'm hungry and tired and he wants me to sit out here all night and watch, I'm not stupid no one followed me." As his head fell on his chest and he was soon asleep. Bill slid his gun from its holster and inched his way along the porch to where Carp was sitting.

Bill smacked Carp alongside the head with the pistol, Carp never made a sound as he fell over; Bill grabbed him and lowered him to the ground.

With his pistol ready, he kicked in the door of the shack. Bart had his head down on the table, with his gun in his hand, at the noise of the door being kicked in; Bart jerked his head up and started to point his pistol at the door. Bill had his pistol aimed at Bart.

"Drop it!" Bart kept raising his gun, Bill shot him in the chest, and the impact of the bullet drove him backwards, with the chair tipping over and the gun flying out of his hand. Bill walked around the table; the hammer was back on his gun, ready to shoot him again, but there was no need. Bart was dead with very little blood. Bill's shot had hit him right in the heart and it stopped pumping instantly the bullet shattered it. Bill saw the sack with the money in it, he picked it up and slung it over his shoulder and went back out the door, there was a bucket of water near the door, and Bill picked it up and dumped it on Carps face. Carp moaned and shook his head, trying to figure out what was going on.

Bill said; "Get up and walk to the barn and saddle a horse for your boss." Carp walked to the barn with Bill behind him, he led the horse out of the barn, and bridled and saddled it as he had been ordered. Bill took the reins and told Carp to head for the shack. He tied the horse to the post, "Now go get your boss out of the shack."

Carp walked into the shack and stared at Bart on the floor.

"Don't just stand there, pick him up and put him over the horse."

Bill looked around and found some rope hanging on a post, he took down the rope and tied Carp's hands behind his back and helped him mount his horse. Bill took the reins of both horses and walked up the hill to the gully where he had left his own horse. Bill mounted the big black, "I better get some money for you two and don't try anything or you will lie across the saddle like your boss." Then Bill headed for town, with Carp and Bart behind him.

— CHAPTER 21 —
KID'S LESSON

Old man Canfield owned one of the largest ranches around Abilene, about twenty miles south east of town. He hollered for his son. "Shawn, I want you to go to town and pick up that new saddle for me". A young man about seventeen came out of his room. "Ok Pa, right after breakfast".

Shawn sat at the table helped himself to eggs, bacon, biscuits and coffee.

"Ya know Pa, I do a lot of work around here and you never pay me." The old man shook his head,

"What the hell you need money for; you charge everything you need to me."

"Pa sometimes a man needs to have his own money."

The old man grumbled. "When you become a man I will start paying you." Then the old man got up and left the table. Shawn got up from the table and went out the door. He walked over to the barn and looked around, then went in through the big doors. Shawn walked over to the toolbox pulled it open and reached down to the bottom of the big box.

Mumbling to out loud, "I'll show him who's a man", as he pulled out a gun and holster , wrapping it a burlap bag, he walked over to the wagon and put the bag under the tarp, hitched up the horse to the wagon and headed for town. About halfway to town, he pulled the horse to a stop, got down and went to the back of the wagon, reached under the tarp and took out his gun. As he strapped on the gun, he looked for a target. About ten feet away was a scrub tree. He took what he thought was a gunfighters stance, drew his gun as fast as he could and fired at the tree. He said out loud, "Wow that was fast and good shooting." Shawn had been practicing for about two months, and thought he was fast. But the truth be told, he was only about as fast as the average cowboy.

Keeping his gun on him he headed for town. About hour later he reached the small town, he stopped in front of Scots saddle and holster shop, pulled on the brake and wrapped the reins around the brake handle. He got down from the wagon and strutted into the saddle shop, thinking he was something.

"Mr. Scot! I'm here to pick up the old man's saddle, the wagons outside, put it under the tarp. Feeling full of himself he headed for the saloon; he walked up the steps and walked through the double batwing doors, strutting as he walked to the bar, "Give me a beer Gus."

Gus being a friend of Shawn's father asked, "What's going on with the gun Shawn?"

"Gus, am I the only man who comes in here with a gun on? Now give me a beer and put it on the old man's bill." Shawn looked around the bar, he saw John Cole sitting at a table.

John was looking at him. "You can't be John Cole the big gun fighter, you're not any older than me". John sipped his cup of coffee, "I hope you didn't come here looking for trouble". Shawn smiled; "Nope I just came in to show people what a real gun gunfighter is like, now get up."

Gus hollered "Shawn don't be stupid!"

"Gus, mind your own business."

"Don't smart mouth me Shawn, or I'll come around this bar and slap the hell out of you."

John looked at the kid, "Why do you want to be a gun fighter?"
"Because I am tired of people treating me like I am just a kid, now get up, or are you a coward?"

John got up from the table. He could see Shawn looking at the bandage on his left hand, "You're lucky it's not your gun hand you hurt Cole."

"Left or right hand it makes no difference kid, I don't know you, and I don't want to kill you, let me ask you something."

"How many hours do you practice with that gun?"

"That's none of your business. Now let's get it done."

"What's the hurry, I'm not going anywhere."

"I practice every chance I get, maybe an hour a day."

Looking into Shawn's eyes, "Well I practice three to four hours every day with both hands, done that for a few years now, and I was taught by one of the best. You can't beat me kid."

Shawn went for his gun, in a split second he was looking at the bore of John's gun, Shawn's hand was just on the butt of the pistol, and his hand froze on the cold metal. "Take your hand off the gun kid, don't make me kill you." With shaking hands Shawn took his hand off the gun, slowly he unbuckled the holster and put it on the bar.

"Take it Gus I don't want it anymore."

John wanted to make the kid feel better, "Now that's what a smart man does, a stupid kid would have tried for it, and would be dead now." Slowly Shawn started to leave the bar.

"Take the gun kid, but leave the holster, a man still needs to protect himself, just never pull it unless you have no choice." Shawn picked up the gun, shoved it in his belt, and looked at John. "Thanks Mr. Cole", and hurried out of the bar.

Gus looked at John,

"Thanks John, he's a good kid; his dad is a friend of mine."

John said, "I knew he was no gunfighter, but I can't take many chances like that, I learned to never underestimate anyone; a kid with a gun can kill you as fast as anyone."

Gus agreed; "I wonder if I should tell his old man?"

John shook his head; "Did you see the fear in his eyes, I don't think he wants to be a gunfighter anymore."

Gus said; "Ok, but if I see him with a gun on again, I will tell the old man how close he came to burying his only son."

CHAPTER 22

THE COLE CABIN

Somewhere in Ohio near the border of Indiana stood the small Cole Cabin, about twenty miles from the town of Blue Ball, in Butler County. Calvin Bradshaw, his wife Caroline and two sons, pulled up in front the Cole home that was occupied by the Johnson family. Ben Johnson was weeding the cornfield, when he saw the wagon and two horsemen heading for the house. Ben was not too concerned, for Butler County did not have a lot of lawlessness. But figured with his wife and children there alone he should get to the house.

Ten year old Timothy was playing on the small patch of grass that was the front yard when he saw people coming and ran inside where Sara and Amy Johnson were making breakfast. "Mom people are coming." Sara looked out the one window the cabin had, "looks like we will have company for breakfast." The three walked out to meet the visitors.

The Bradshaw family pulled in front of the house just as Ben arrived in from the field.

Ben had his shotgun with him but it was pointed at the ground. "Step down and have breakfast with us." Calvin got down from the wagon. The two boys dismounted and spread out from their father, their mother stayed in the wagon.

All had pistols strapped on. "Nice spread you have here, I been looking it over for a few days now, I decided to buy it from you."

Ben shook his head, "Not for sale, and not mine to sell."

"Oh who owns it?" asked Calvin.

Ben did not like how this was going, "The Cole brothers do." Bradshaw said "If you don't own it why are you here."

Ben said; "You are a bit nosey friend, I think it be best if you water your horses and move on." Calvin rested his hand on the butt of his pistol and so did his boys.

"If you are living here, you can sell it, I'm going to give you five hundred in gold."

Ben shook his head, "Not interested and it is worth five times that much."

Calvin Bradshaw pulled a paper out of his pocket, "I have the agreement all made out, and you will sign it now. I would not want your family to get hurt now, would you?"

"The only one who will get hurt is you; this scatter gun will blow you apart." Bradshaw said to his sons, "If he shoots me, Jubal you shoot him, Sid you shoot the woman and the boy, save the other one you can use her for a while."

Sara took her husband's arm, "Ben lets go, and when the Cole's come back they will take care of it." Ben took the paper and pencil and signed the paper.

"Where's the money Ben asked".

Bradshaw laughed, "Well you got it, it says so right here. I received five hundred dollars in gold, from Calvin Bradshaw, signed Ben Johnson. Now get your belongings and leave."

Ben said; "You think you're going to get away with this, I guess you don't know who the Coles are, but you will find out in due time." Ben and his family packed and left, and headed for town. Upon reaching Blue Ball, Ben sent a message to Abilene, where John said he could be reached. Explaining what had taken place.

─ CHAPTER 23 ─
HOME TO OHIO

The year is 1939; the old man sat in his rocking chair and said; "Well now, you know the life story of your Grandparents and your Uncle Bill". One of the younger grandkids asked "Then everything we heard about you is true?"

John smiled; "Well to my recollection, what I told you is true, what others say, I cannot say."

"You did not tell us how the Johnson's became like family." John closed his eyes as he thought back. "Well when your great grandparents died, me being a young man, I wanted to see some of the west. I let the Johnson's use the farm, with the understanding that I would be back someday."

It was a warm quiet afternoon in Abilene, John was out making his rounds as acting deputy for Sheriff Pete. His thoughts wandered to his brother Bill, was he having this quiet a life as a bounty hunter.? Then almost as if someone had read his mind Rock came out of the Telegraph Office waving a message at him. "looks like your brother and yourself have some sorting out to do at home" John read the brief message, crumpling it up in anger when he realized what the Bradshaw's had done. He went to the Telegraph office and sent wires to Bill the places that they had agreed upon, telling him he would meet him in Cane Creek, Missouri. He told him he would be on his way as soon as he and Jenny could get married

John ran over to Mary's, Jenny came out of the kitchen wiping her hands on her apron; she looked alarmed "What's happened John?" "There's trouble at home, seems like a family of crooks have taken our home place over and kicked the Johnson's out" he explained. "I promised Bill we would meet him over in Cane Creek as soon as possible and sort this out. But before we can leave you and me need to find the preacher, I ain't about to leave you behind" John looked at her anxiously "If that's okay with you, that is"? Jenny pulled off her apron and hugged him, "Yes, yes, you go sort the preacher and I'll go get Mom to help me arrange everything"

John went across the street to find the preacher, on the way he bumped into Sheriff Murphy, "Look Sheriff, a problem has cropped up; I got to leave as soon as I can get ready for the trip back to Ohio. You are getting fat and lazy anyways, with me doing all the work."

Pete said; "I will hate to see you go John, but I understand."

With that done John arranged for the Preacher to marry him and Jenny the next day.

After the short ceremony in front of the friends the couple had in town, John noticed Rock was very sitting off to one side on his own and very quiet.

"Rock, would you like to come with us and help us work the farm?" Rock became teary eyed and said, "I would love to I thought you would never ask."

John clapped his friend on the shoulder "well now that's settled Rock, I have to ask you something, I have not been nosey, but I can see you are sweet on Mary." Rock just smiled.

I said, "Wow if you and Mary get hitched you will be my father-in-law." He laughed.

"You must have a name besides Rock; we are not going to call Mary, Mrs. Rock."

"Well my given name is Joe Vandervort."

"That's a good name, but I think I'll call you Rocky Joe" John laughed.

Rock shrugged "Rocky Joe is ok, as long as you don't call me," Old Joe." That the two friends laughed and it was settled, Rocky Joe was his name from that day on.

John figured they had about a hundred miles to go before they could get to a Railway station. He bought a wagon and supplies, Crenshaw gave him a good deal on a wagon and horse to pull it. The first two days of travel were easy. The small group made good time, about ten to fifteen miles a day, on the third day John heard a lot of yelling. He told Rock to hold up and rode close to a top of a hill Dismounting he let the reins fall to the ground, Amber would not move, John crawled to the top of the hill, not wanting to skyline himself. There were still Indians around and one still had to be careful. Relieved he saw it was a trail herd and not Indians. No longer worried about Indians, John stood up and waved Rock on. It was not long before the trail herd spotted them. A rider approached with caution at first, but when he saw the wagon and women, he relaxed and rode up to John. "How do friend, I am Charlie Hill, owner of this herd."

John reached over and took his hand. "The names John Cole" he pointed over his shoulder to the wagon "this is my family, we are heading for Ohio."

"Well Mr. Cole, it is getting late and we are going to make camp, you can spend the night with us and eat supper with us if you like."

"We would be happy to spend the night with you, the women folk would be happy to help your cook with supper."

John told the family what was going on, Mary and Jenny were happy to be with more people, safety in numbers. "Rock, pull the wagon over near their chuck wagon". Jenny, would you and your Mom help the cook with dinner?" They both said yes as John had known they would.

Rock unhitched the wagon horse while John unsaddled Amber, he ground hitched her near the stream and some good grass. The women helped with supper. John and Rock walked over to the campfire and introduced themselves.

One of the men did not seem too friendly, "Cole, names sounds familiar, were you a marshal in Adobe Walls?"

"No that was my brother Bill." The man said no more. Rock and John got a mug of coffee each and sat down by the fire.

"I did not catch your name friend, do you know my brother?"

"That's because I didn't give it, saw your brother but did not know him."

"No need to be unfriendly Dirk" said Charlie Hill. Dirk said nothing, but John noticed him always looking at Jenny and that did not upset him, she is a very pretty lady and men on a trail drive don't see woman very often, but he was going to keep his eye on him.

The cook hollered "Come and get it before I throw it away." Everyone got up and got plates food, John noticed Dirk was getting a little too close to Jenny, and so walked over and stood beside her. Dirk filled his plate and brushed into Jenny as he walked away. John said nothing but he took his plate and walked over to the campfire and sat across from him. Dirk gave him a smirk. John looked at him and said quietly; "I am a guest here and don't want any trouble, but stay away from my wife."

Dirk put his plate down and stood up, "And what if I don't?"

John jumped up and faced him "Then they will bury you here."

"Just because your brother is a gunfighter, don't mean you are." "Like I said I am a guest here, but you had your warning, I won't tell you again."

"That will be all Dirk," snapped Charlie. Dirk took his plate and walked away, sulking. Rock got up and walked over to our wagon, John knew he was going to keep an eye on Jenny and her mother; Rock was getting pretty friendly with Mary.

"I appreciate you trying to avoid trouble here," said Charlie. "I am close to cutting Dirk loose, he's been nothing but trouble since I hired him."

"I understand men looking at a pretty woman, especially when they been on a drive for a long time, but if he bothers my wife again, I won't overlook it a second time."

Dirk walked over to the Cole's wagon, Jenny had her back to him, and he walked up behind her and put his arms around her. Thinking it was John she leaned back into him. Rock saw him with his arms around Jenny.

Rock "yelled what the hell you think you're doing." Jenny turned and saw it was not John and screamed. Rock grabbed Dirk and spun him around, Dirk being a young man was stronger and faster than Rock. "Why you old fart" and then he hit Rock a hard right to Rock's jaw. Rock fell backwards and was out cold.

John heard Jenny scream and ran over to her, and yelled "You son of a bitch." Dirk turned and faced John with his hand close to his gun. Jenny told John later she never seen him so mad. John never took my eyes off of Dirk, He told Jenny to move aside. Dirk had that grin on his face again.

"I warned you not to go near my wife, now draw your gun." Dirk just stood there with his hand near his gun not making a move for it.

"I told you draw your gun!" "If you don't, I am going to kill you anyways."

Dirk went for his gun, as his hand touched the butt of his pistol, he felt something hit him in the chest and knock him backwards, He looked at John with eyes that could not believe what had happened, then fell on his back with still wide open eyes and knew no more, or what no living man knows.

Jenny ran to John crying, "Why can't they leave you alone John, they always make you use the gun, I know it's not your fault."

"It will be different in Ohio" he told her.

The other cowboys were standing around talking, one said; Dirk was pretty good with a gun, but I never saw anything like that kid. Charlie told the men to break it up. "Cole I know it was not your fault, and Dirk got what was coming to him, you gave him fair warning, But I think in the morning it would be better if you went your own way, Women on a cattle drive just never work out."

John nodded "I understand Mr. Hill, and I am sorry to have caused you to lose a man."

John woke up before first light, though John and Jenny were married, John slept under the wagon with old Rock. John rapped on the wagon to wake Jenny and her mom, "Time to get ready to move out." Jenny and her mom started breakfast, coffee bacon and biscuits. John looked towards the east as the sun just started to rise, he walked over and gave Jenny a kiss, " looks like it will be a hot one, we should get moving before it gets too hot, we still have about sixty miles to go, The train will be a much easier ride than the wagon."

Jenny asked, "Are we traveling with Mr. Hill?" John shook his head no. "John I know it was not your fault, but it seems it is always the gun."

"Jen, you know I try not to put myself in that position, But I won't allow anyone to put their hands on you, or your mother. A man has to protect his family. I'm just glad I am able to do it." After breakfast John hitched up the horse to the wagon, while Rock helped Jenny and Mary get ready. They said goodbye to Mr. Hill and his men. John rode out front on Amber and Rock drove the wagon together they headed out along the prairie

Later that night sitting by the campfire and having coffee, as the woman cleaned up the dishes. Rock said to John.

"I'm going to ask Mary if she will marry me."

"That comes as no surprise, when are you thinking of asking her?"

"I'm going to ask her tonight."

John smiled; "Now is as good as time as any Rock."

"With a shaky voice rock said; "But I'm scared John, what if she says no."

"Well you can always pick up a rock and stone her." John slapped his leg and laughed.

"Not funny John."

Mary and Jenny looked over at the two men.

"Want to let us in on what is so funny" asked Mary. John was still laughing, "Maybe later".

Rock asked John if he would take Jenny for a stroll so he could be alone with Mary.

John got up and walked over to the wagon. "Jen let's take a walk and look at the moonlight."

Jenny put her arm in John's, and as they walked away, "Is something up, or are you feeling frisky."

John smiled, "I always feel frisky when I am around you. But that's not it this time."

"Ok John what's going on?"

"Well, how would you like to have Rock as your new daddy?" And he laughed.

"I knew Rock had feelings for mom, and if it makes mom happy then I will be happy."

— CHAPTER 24 —
THE FARM

When they reached the railroad they sold the wagon and horse, and loaded Amber in an empty cattle car, and then took the train to Missouri. They waited for Bill at Cane Creek, he showed up a week later. John and Rock had already bought a wagon and two horses to haul it, with Amber tied to the back of the wagon they headed for Ohio. Bill was in a hurry to get to the cabin and move the Bradshaw's off the farm; John told him they should give the law a chance first. Bill agreed, but said he would put up with no nonsense. Ohio had more law than most of the other places, but the further west you went the less law there was and it was still the way of the gun. It seemed to take forever to reach the brothers town of Blue Ball, when they got there the first thing they did was settle Jenny and Mary into a hotel, as John was leaving, Jen said, "The gun John, you told me you would not need it here." John nodded and took off his gun and put it away'. "Bill was outside waiting for him." 'Together they walked over to the Sheriff's office, opened the door and walked in." A man was sitting at a desk, he looked up and said; "Most people knock before they come in." Bill paid no attention and asked, "Where is Sheriff Morgan." Rising from his chair, the man said, "Sheriff Morgan retired a while ago, I'm Sheriff Brown, Clem Brown, who are you and what can I do for you?"

"We are Bill and John Cole; we want to know what you are going to do about our farm."

"Ben Johnson told me you would be coming back, I heard of you boys, gunfighters, well there won't be any of that here."

Bill snapped. "Did you also hear that we were both sheriff's before we came back here?" That's why we came to see you first, but one way or another, the Bradshaw's will leave our property."

"I already told the Johnsons, that the Bradshaw's had a paper showing he sold them the property". John said "Sheriff that the property was not theirs to sell, you need to move them or we will."

"We will have to let the judge decide that." The sheriff said. Bill replied shortly "you've had a long enough time to have done that." "Don't you boys start any trouble." Bill was angry and let the sheriff know it, "I've told you once already the Bradshaw's will leave one way or another; you got two days to move them off our property sheriff, that's all." The brothers left the sheriff's office and went to the hotel to get the family and walked down the street to the first eating place they saw, after they had all eaten dinner they walked around the town, and let the ladies do some shopping. Old Rock said;" I think I will go have me a beer after we settle the womenfolk back at the hotel." "I'm going back with Jenny anyways so you go along Rock, Me and Bill will catch up with you over there."

After they had Jenny and Mary settled in safely John and Bill went looking for the saloon that Rock was in. down the street a little way John saw a sign "Hard Rock saloon." he laughed and told Bill, "I'm sure that is Rock will be." The brothers strolled down the dusty street to the saloon, as they entered, Bill stopped and waited for his eyes to adjust to the dim light, even though Blue Ball was a peaceful place, old habits are hard to break. They saw Rock at the bar and walked over to him. John put three nickels on the bar and said, "Three beers". Old Rock said; "Remember John, I promised only a beer after lunch and dinner, this one makes two." "Today is an exception."

"There are no exceptions John." "Rock came a long ways since I dunked him in that watering trough." Once again Rock surprised John by motioning him closer Speaking low he said; "You see the three men at the table to the right of us." John glanced swiftly over to the table and said; "What about them:" Rock said, "Them's the Bradshaw's." Rock always seemed to know what and who everyone is. The men saw John looking at them; the three got up and walked over to the bar, the older man said; "Are you the Coles?"

Bill turned and faced them, "What business is it to you who we are?" "Well I am Calvin Bradshaw and these are my boys, if you think you are going to get us off our farm, we might as well settle it now." Bill told them "If you want to die, then just go for those guns. John was not armed, and did not want Bill to go against three guns. "Bill we told the sheriff two days, "Bradshaw if you're not gone in two days we will be out to see you."

"We're not going anywhere's, see you in two days." The older boy, with a smirk on his face said "I can't wait."

Bill said quietly "Don't be in such a hurry to die boy." The old man said "See you in two days", and they left the saloon.

John, Bill and Rock finished their beers and left the saloon, back in the hotel room John told Jenny what had happened. "Do you think they will be gone when you get out there John?" she asked with a worried look on her face. "We can only hope they are my dear, I don't want any more trouble now I have you to watch out for too"

Two days went by fast, the sheriff done nothing to remove the Bradshaw's, so John and Bill were getting ready to go out to the farm.

John kissed Jenny and walked over to the wall where his gun was hanging; he strapped it on, tied it down then walked out the door."

As they walked to the stable, the sheriff stopped them, "Don't go out there boys." Bill looked at him, "You had your two days Sheriff, now get out of my way." John watched the sheriff's eyes.

"Don't even think of it Brown, the Bradshaw's are scum, don't die for the likes of them". "Look Sheriff, my brother and me have always been on the right side of the law. Our mother and father spent their lives' on that farm, and are buried there. No one is going to steal it from us."

As they saddled and mounted their horses, they saw Rock running towards them with a shotgun in his hand.

"Forget it Rock, not your fight."

"Sure it is John."

"Rock if you want to help, you stay and watch out for the women that would take a load off my mind."

"Ok son if that's what you want me to do."

"Thanks Rock", they headed out of town to the farm. As they got close to the farm, Bill said; "We got to be careful, if we just ride up to the house they will just bushwhack us, lets come in from the south side behind the barn, and we can sit and wait for someone to come out. They rode around to the back of the barn and dismounted and waited till the men came out.

All three of the Bradshaw's walked towards the barn. When they got to about twenty feet from the doorway, John and Bill stepped out from around the building. The older Bradshaw boy started for his gun, as his hand touched the butt of his pistol; he was looking at two pistols aimed at him. Bill said; "Go on draw it, and die." The old man said: "No! Take your hand off the gun." Slowly the older boy took his hand off his gun, and moved his hand away from his body. John looked at old man "Bradshaw, We are going to be fair about this; we are going to buy the farm back for the same five hundred dollars in gold that you paid Ben Johnson."

"And what if I say no?" asked Bradshaw. "Then you get the same choice you gave Ben Johnson and his family." John reached into his shirt pocket and pulled out a slip of paper. "I have the bill of sale all made out, he threw it in the ground at Bradshaw's feet, sign it."

Old man Bradshaw picked up the paper and signed it, and then handed it to John, "Where is the five hundred in gold he asked." John smiled and said: "You got it, it says it right here, I Calvin Bradshaw received five hundred dollars in gold, from John Cole." "Now drop your guns and get."

"What about our belongings"? Bill said "You're lucky we even let you take your horses, Get your woman in the wagon now and move out. If you come back you and your sons will die." Bill kept a watchful eye on them as they hitched the wagon and headed out.

John headed back to town to go get the family, leaving Bill to watch the place. Jenny and Mary sure would be pleased it had been done with no killing When John got back to town the sheriff was waiting outside the hotel " did you kill them?" Showing him the bill of sale John laughed and said "The Bradshaw's saw the error of their ways".

Jenny was waiting anxiously; he explained to her what had happened. Before they headed out to the farm they went and found Ben Johnson and told him to get his family ready, that they had a cabin to build for them.

━ CHAPTER 25 ━
BRADSHAW'S RETURN

The female voice was soft, but loud enough for John's old ears to hear. "It's getting late John; it's time to come in." John chuckled, "When Grandma Jen speaks, I still jump, just not as high."

"Grandpa did the Bradshaw's ever come back?"

Yes Johnny, they're still here."

"Where do they live Grandpa?"

"There Up on Boot Hill, Johnny."

"Can you tell me what happened to them Grandpa?"

"As I remember how you great uncle Bill told me." "Bill and I figured we had seen the last of the Bradshaw's, but that was not so."

"A week or so after we took the farm back, great uncle Bill went into town to buy lumber for the Johnson's and his cabin, I knew why Bill wanted his own cabin." John smiled, as he thought back. Uncle Bill had hopes of marrying, your great aunt Amy."

"Well Bill headed to town in the wagon, as he headed down the hill just before yellow creek, the three Bradshaw's, rode out of the pines three abreast, they stopped in front of Bill." Old man Bradshaw did the talking, as his two boys, sat smirking with their hands near their guns.

"We have a paper we would like you to sign" he told Bill. Bill replied,

"The only paper I will sign is the one telling the sheriff how you three died."

The older son said; "You think you're good enough to get all three of us?"

"I know at least two of you will die."

The younger boy went for his gun, Bill drew his colt and shot him in the chest before his gun was out of its holster, then rolled out of the wagon to the ground and shot the other boy.

"Grandpa, young John asked, "Why did he not shoot the father first"?

"As Bill told me later, if they killed him he wanted the old man to regret losing his two sons. Now do you want to hear the rest or not?"

"Yes Grandpa."

"Bill turned to face the father, and saw the rifle pointed at him, he knew he was too late, Bill heard the crack of the rifle, but felt no bullet, he saw old man Bradshaw fall backwards of his horse.

Bill got up off the ground and made sure all three were dead or out of commission. Then he heard the horse come over the hill towards him.

Bill saw it was Rock, with a rifle in his hand. How Rock knew Bill would be in danger we will never know. Rock had a habit of always knowing things, if you ask him how he knows he will only shrug, and say "Beats me". "A better friend, Bill and me will never have.

Grandpa just two more questions, "Asked John Jr. "do you still have your gun?"

"Yes Johnny, I gave it to your dad. When he was old enough I taught him how to use it, as time went by there was no need for a gun anymore, so he put it away in the barn under lock and key, it is the gun you hear me shoot every morning, Someday I am sure he will give it to you for a keepsake, so you can remember your old Grandpa."

"Grandpa did all our horses come from the black stallion and the appaloosa, that great uncle Bill got from the Indians?"

"That was the start of them, along with my Amber and Bills big black." John's eyes filled up as he thought of Amber." "That's enough for tonight Johnny; your old Grandpa is tired".

"Grandpa, just one more thing."

"Yes Johnny."

"I love you Grandpa."

"I love you too Johnny."

John slowly got up from the rocking chair, and went into the house. He turned and looked out at his sons and grandchildren. Then said; "I am a lucky man Jen." Jenny put her arm around his waist, "And I'm a lucky woman, John."

Before going to bed young John Cole Jr. the 3rd wrote down in his journal all that his grandfather had told him. That night he dreamed of Gunfighters and Indians.

CHAPTER 26
FIRST LESSON

The following morning John got out of bed, walking slowly with stiff aching joints; he put on his Levis, denim shirt and boots, leaned over and kissed Jenny. He went into the kitchen and made coffee in the new coffee pot, he waited as the kitchen filled with the rich smell of fresh coffee brewing, when it was ready he filled his cup and went outside, looking up at the orange globe rising in the east. Talking out loud "Looks like another beautiful day." He turned and looked up the hill at the old oak tree, with the white picket fence around it, then walked up the hill to the family cemetery. Looking at the first grave he said out loud, as he did every morning. "William & Mira Cole. 1877." Then looked at the next one, "Eileen Jenny Cole 1882- 1884 the apple of my eye." Then far over to Johns right. There were two more head stones. "You were a great friend to me Rock." He read out loud "Joe Vandervort 1905, and Mary Vandervort 1908." The sun was warming his back and a chorus of birds had begun to greet the new day. John bowed his head and said a short prayer then headed back down the hill for the barn, inside the doorway, Bill was waiting for him. "Morning John", he took out a key and opened the cabinet on the barn wall, inside hanging on pegs were two holsters with guns in them, one was right handed and one was left, they strapped them on, and walked out the back door of the barn, heading for the old tree, where their dad had taught them how to shoot a long time ago. John looked at Bill and said; "Think you can beat me yet." Bill laughed and said; "Who cares, let's have some fun, while we still can." On the tree were the new targets with the bull's-eye in the center. Bill faced the target, with a smooth and steady hand he drew his colt and fired, one in the center of the bulls-eye and one just on the edge. "Not bad for an old man:" laughed John. John drew with the same smoothness as his brother and fired two shots in the center of the Bulls- eye. "Like you told me a long time ago brother, make your shots count." Quietly John said; "Is he watching?" Bill said, "Do cows give milk." I think I will ask my son if I can teach young John to shoot." They fired a few more shots, and then headed for the house for breakfast that Jenny and Amy, were cooking. From the hayloft where he watched every day, was John Cole Jr. the 3rd. writing everything they did and said in his journal?

— CHAPTER 27 —
EPILOGUE

The year was 1955; sitting in a bookstore, at a table with a stack of books was John Cole Jr. the 3rd. beside on the table laid a worn holster and pistol.

While signing a book for a customer, he was asked,

"Is this a true story or fiction?" John looked at the man. "This is a true story of two brothers who were gunfighters in the old west, as told to me by my Grandfather and his friends."

The customer looked interested and turned the book over in his hands, flicking through the first page or two.

"If you want to know what it was really like back then, buy my book. If you just want a shoot'em up book, then buy the old dime novels over there."

The man said, "I will buy yours, if you will you sign the book for me. Is that your grandfather's gun?"

John smiled; "Yes my Dad gave it to me, and my grandfather taught me how to use it."

The big yellow dog lying next to John, got up and sniffed the man, the man jumped back afraid of the big dog.

"Amber come here and lay down."

With his coffee in his right hand, John took a sip and signed the book, with his left hand. John thanked the man and started to hand him the book; changing his mind he opened the book once more. Inside the front cover he wrote a footnote for the man.

A true story of my grandfather John Cole, the fastest gun of his time and my great uncle Bill Cole, who was well known and feared as a gunfighter, as told to me by my Granddad, it was my Great uncle Bill who taught John Cole, his younger brother the fast Draw.

The Left Hand Gun
By
John Cole Jr. the 3rd